SKELMERSDALE

FICTION RESERVE STOCK LL 60

AUTHOR	CLASS

TITLE

THE CLOUD OF DUST

Charlie Boxer was born in 1961 and grew up in London. In 1985 he launched a magazine for teenagers on historical subjects that are not taught in schools, writing and publishing each of the issues himself. Charlie Boxer lives in London with the subject of this book and their two sons.

Charlie Boxer

THE CLOUD
OF DUST

V

VINTAGE

Published by Vintage 2001

2 4 6 8 10 9 7 5 3 1

First published in Great Britain by
Jonathan Cape 2000

Vintage
Random House, 20 Vauxhall Bridge Road,
London SW1V 2SA

Random House Australia (Pty) Limited
20 Alfred Street, Milsons Point, Sydney
New South Wales 2061, Australia

Random House New Zealand Limited
18 Poland Road, Glenfield,
Auckland 10, New Zealand

Random House (Pty) Limited
Endulini, 5A Jubilee Road, Parktown 2193,
South Africa

The Random House Group Limited Reg. No. 954009
www.randomhouse.co.uk

A CIP catalogue record for this book
is available from the British Library

ISBN 0 09 928564 9

Pa   le
pr   s.
Th   n-

Many are the secret ways we relish pain.

We can never reveal this; we are more secretive about our taste for cradling hurt within ourselves than about anything else.

Especially are we careful that our relations with others should not appear as masochistic as they indubitably are.

But first love can surprise us. We are not prepared for the suddenness with which we are exposed.

And having revealed everything in those moments, embarrassed and inspired, it sometimes happens that we do, once, publicly affirm the divinity of pain. And from love extract only the creamy astringency of rejection.

This is my story.

In a letter which he sent me when I was seventeen years old, my friend xxxx warned me that love would soon consume me completely. Anxious for my security, he wanted to tell me that there was no worse protection against the wounds of love than a reliance on the quality of selflessness.

Nor did this beautiful and brilliant man give me

more advice than was implicit in this. He emphasised his warning with a terrible flourish: 'The bloody flux seize upon you, the cursed sharp inflammations of wild fire, as slender and thin as cow's hair strengthened with quicksilver, enter into your fundament, and like those of Sodom and Gomorrah, may you fall into sulphur, fire and bottomless pits, in case you do not firmly believe all that I relate.'

The threat overwhelmed the caution. I did not know how to believe either. I put the letter, carefully, into my drawer, to keep for ever. These letters that follow are the record of the wisdom of his foresight.

Though the letters deal with real events, they were rewritten some twenty years later, the originals being quite lost.

THE
CLOUD
OF
DUST

9th September

Dear M,

I have just arrived and been shown my room. It is very comfortable. Mary and Tom are friendly and have welcomed me warmly. There is a large double bed in my room; I have barely ever slept in one before, and on top of it lies stretched a gloomy brown woollen counterpane. When I saw it, and the oilcloth on the table by the bed, I knew that Mary and Tom had been careful that I should not receive too effusive a welcome, that a pretence would remain throughout my stay here that I was to be purely a lodger, an inconvenience in their household, and useful and valued only in so far as I paid my rent to them. How far these formalities will go beyond keeping my room dowdy and my rent-paying ceremony awkward I do not know, but they are keen as children to have this strange person in their house. Mary had roasted a chicken for my arrival; their daughter Effie – who is about eight or nine – was delighted with the celebration. Afterwards Tom showed me his books, and his printing press, and talked for a long time about his plans to leave his teaching job and become a publisher of poetry. I did nothing to deserve these kindnesses, or these confidences.

The house is in a suburban street. They are all detached and large, the front doors always left open whenever someone is in, each one having a glass inner door to keep the cold out and let the light of occupation shine into the street. And yet, from my bedroom window I look directly out on distant hills from where a keen and lively wind blows. It is wonderfully sweet and wild, this air. I have not smelt anything like it before. I have not felt anything like it before. I have not had anything like it forced into me before! The tang of a Scottish autumn storm must be one of the great things of the world, I knew this as soon as I felt it in my face. This, if nothing else, makes me extremely happy. I am excited to be here. I know no one at all. I come at a moment of great anxiety, doubt and uncertainty; this is all very good. The venture is as great as it could ever be for me.

10th September

Dear Paul,

So here I am in Edinburgh. I think a lot about you. You are sweet and kind and thoughtful, patient in your understanding, indulgent in your handling of the gripes and complaints of others; you are a marvel, a god of friends. And here I am in this place, having no company but my own, no person to talk to, and I miss talking, I miss being with you, I miss that keen uncertain approach you make to the friends you see each day, that hesitant re-establishing of interest and affection each time the mouth opens, that delicious fear of hurting your friend with a banality, that continual deepening of estimation that overcoming banality brings. All these things I love about being with you. Love is part horror; I depend on you to keep me inspired with the holy dread of mutual affection.

And now alone, great waves of scheming thought approach the borders of my brain, and I speak aloud to the curtains and the window panes what I might declaim to you were we together and dawn breaking over the pale rooftops of London as I remember it was the last time we said goodbye. The intensity of my recollections of you murmurs in a sort of continual fugue of farewell. As the intimacy dies so the affection flares up.

This removal from my habitual world, so abrupt and so complete, is like a sort of death. I am perched in this citadel of the north, high up in the clouds, and I look down on my family and friends through the sleet of previously unremembered occasions.

All the names, figures, shapes of my vanished boyhood cloud around me. Everything and every person I have loved I remember, and how secretly I loved them, and how by this secrecy love consolidated my despair about myself. I think of everyone I have loved as germs of those I will one day love. Items lost and adored; burnished into a sort of hard-skinned permanence so the memory becomes a sheen on which all the things yet to come can be found reflected.

I rhapsodised to myself today about my early life, watching countless souls dancing upon their little spot of ground. And I who watched them remained a vapour, a cloud of insubstantial dust moving like a swarm of midges, bodily, across wide distances of time and space, buzzing, loving, adoring. I mean loving things, but not being a thing myself. A being that loved in secret, never taking shape, or form, never growing into a definite person.

And I think all these things while a bitter Scottish storm beats merrily against my window.

P.S. 11th September. You must have seen my family's troubles in the newspapers. My father's affair with, allegedly, the most glamorous woman in the country, a scandal on every front page, the public speculation over a possible divorce from his wife of twenty-five years. You can imagine what this means for all of us; the excitement for him and the mortification of my mother who sits alone in an empty house, daughter, son and wayward husband all gone. I can hardly speak to her when I telephone. Such has been the tenderness of our relationship that it was inevitable that when I left home I would be overcome with anxiety for her. The fact that Dad has so publicly fallen in love with another woman compounds my own secret remorse for my abandonment of her.

She does not complain, but her dejection is palpable within her bravery. If I were to worry for her too much I would only give her more grief and worry. So I reassure her that I am all right by being insensitive.

Life, alone up here, has become like a strange sucking away of actual facts. The sheath of unpredictable familiarity has been punctured, and the atmosphere of my identity is slowly leaking away. To be alone for the first time, and have the crescendo of other people's sufferings and griefs drowning out all the tender musings you were preparing for yourself. I am inert and anxious, responsive and indifferent, caught in a wild erratic alternation. A rupture with self-absorption, oh! it is with glazed eyes that you first look through your own passion.

14th September

Dear M,

How are you? I hope you are well. It was lovely talking to you on the phone yesterday. I thought you sounded very well. I was sad about your news though, and wish I could be with you. However, I am sure everything will start to feel better in a while. Things will become normal again. I think I like it here. I don't know anyone at all, but everyone is kind and friendly. I have been wandering around and taking my bearings of the city. Yesterday I went and looked at the house where you were born. It was so white and grand and impersonal; if you come up and stay we shall go and look at it together. It is full of solicitors' offices now, maybe they could be of some use to you! The bookshops are the best things, so far. They are very cheap and the books are varied and interesting, more so than London second-hand bookshops. I have been buying about five or six a day, all of them books I have wanted to read and never before found. I take them home and then read only one or two pages. It can be a disappointment, discovering things you have long hoped to possess. I work hard in my room and then when I hear Mary pottering about downstairs I go and take a rest and lie on the floor in the kitchen. This tickles Mary, who is kind. She smiles down on me in a way that is both prim and indulgent; she is surprised by me and also amused by her surprise. While she makes coffee for us both she asks me questions. She is pleased I am enjoying my work, and pleased to hear me say I am happy and believes me in so far as she can see I am relaxed, but she still looks dubiously down on me where I lie on the linoleum. She wants me to confide in her about all the mischief I mean to get up to. She likes to suspect already that I am hiding many details of my nightly debauches. I will certainly disappoint her . . .

16th September

Dear Paul,

Your letter was quite extraordinary. It over-whelmed me. I could do nothing yesterday but think about it, and consider what a poor reply I could make. So I have given up sending you anything so fine, and am lazily writing this from my counterpane. I never expected that separation would so intensify our affection for each other. I have never thought of you as frequently, or as fondly, as now; and only you, you alone of every-one I love or care for – to the exclusion of all other friends – have become fixed in my thoughts. But I fear already how this growing dependence on your memory allows me to luxuriate in list-less solitude.

I read books, forgotten, neglected books. I browse in bookshops and if I find something that I am sure you would never read then I pick it up, take it home, and see how well it pleases me. This way I came to discover the poetry of Ossian, which you would despise. I will not bore you with its dim, lunatic grandeur, only that it makes me feel how sad it is to be a boy, and not to have loved with passion at all, even in pretence, and to be sitting here, alone on these grey afternoons and reading through rubbishy old literary antiques. The lonely choose the most earnest distractions.

Ossian is a famous old literary fraud. It was claimed to be a cycle of songs found alive in the mouths of Hebridean bards late in the eighteenth century. As such it was passed off on to the Romantic world, after translation into flowery English, as authentic pre- or anti-Christian Gaelic poetry. It was hugely popular for a while, and looked upon with all the excitement as if it had been the work of a Western European Homer. Here, I've decided now to copy a bit for you, just so as you can conceive how it affects me, to be absorbed in this sad old trash!

I sit by the mossy fountain; on the top of the hill of winds. One tree is rustling above me. Dark waves roll over the heath. The lake is troubled below. The deer descend from the hill. It is mid-day: but all is silent. Sad are my thoughts alone. Dids't thou but appear, O my love, a wanderer on the heath! Thy hair floating on the wind behind thee: thy bosom heaving on the sight; thine eyes full of tears for thy friends, whom the mist of the hill had concealed! Thee I would comfort, my love, and bring thee to thy father's house.

But is it she that appears, like a beam of light on the heath? Bright as the moon in autumn, as the sun in a summer storm, comest thou lovely maid

over rocks, over mountains to me? – she speaks: but
how weak her voice! Like the breeze in the weeds
in the pool. Hark!

To be interested in fakes is the last word in boredom, and desperate self-concealment. It is partly being in a northern city, but it is remarkable how my own loneliness and the soporific charms of this poetry conspire together to make me feel the deep influence of Ossian on the world. No one reads it now, but I see the ripples across the surface of our world that this fantasy inspired. I read it, and I see the way glib fashion conditions our sentiments so profoundly. Ossian launched that mawkish blindness to the real world which is responsible for so much of our boredom and listlessness. Ossian excited a strain of delusive silliness that persists today in fraudulence and complacency.

After thinking like this, I remember who I am. My thoughts suddenly leap towards you.

Sunday afternoon

Dear M,

It is very domestic here. Mary cooked lunch today and several of their friends came round. We lit a fire and sat around on the carpet, talking about articles in magazines and politics. Their friends were very scathing of my opinions – which were ridiculously mild for their tastes – but Tom and Mary could not be sweeter. Tom has this schoolmasterly eagerness to understand exactly what I mean which is too good-hearted to be condescending. Mary afterwards said she thought I talked much more sense than all the rot the others were saying. I find it a little sad; their marriage, Mary told me, is not going well. She says she does not know how much longer they will stay together.

Mary says that you have been phoning her up and asking about me. She says that you are a little worried I am lonely. She hints that I'd better become more enterprising if she is to lie on my behalf. 'I want to see you go out more often,' she says. 'I want more girls to phone up for you!' She is keen for a little conspiracy between us I think. Sometimes when she has come back from a shift at the hospital she stays wearing her nurse's outfit. Her manner changes, and she becomes more abrupt and direct.

She rattled the door when I was having a bath last night, and came in and out, carrying towels and sheets to and from the cupboard. 'Don't mind me,' she said blithely, 'I've seen everything.' And then looking down on me in the bath she said, 'You're very handsome, you know.' I found this very touching; there was not the remotest possibility I could mistake this piece of encouragement for anything else.

It's very interesting to live with a strange family. You discover not only the subtlety of other people's intelligence but also their trust in your own. I feel there is not the remotest possibility there could ever be a misunderstanding between me and them. They are so kind, both of them; the tragedy is that their goodness – he a schoolteacher, she a nurse – has the effect of making their lives uneventful and un-exciting, which is all I think their marriage suffers from.

20th September

Dear Paul,

Though we are far apart we lie on our beds together! We remember and forget. We establish constellations of memory within ourselves, pinpricks upon the veil of oblivion, each stab against the darkness too small to fade. This is our identity for eternity, it has been cast, these constellations of light we shall look to in later life, they shall be our guide, and yet, and yet, I am almost no longer myself on these lonely grey afternoons. I still pore over old books and find myself sharing with the dead a host of elaborate, artificial joys.

I think of you partly in honour of a man I love, partly to distract myself from the tedium of my own circumstances: friendless, uninterested in my work, consigned to remain in this foreign city, uninterested in the people I look at, and worried that I might be preparing myself to lead a life of perpetually concealed boredom. What next?

24th September

Dear M,

I am not sure where to send this. You must tell me exactly what is happening to you. Have you moved out yet, or are you still at home? Your letter is so cheerful. It is an awkward blunt question, but are you concealing some news from me? What arrangement have you come to with Dad? Is he giving you money? Do you speak to him? Are you going to be all right? Is anyone helping you cope? I can no longer bear to look at the newspapers for fear of coming on some horrid piece of gossip about you or Dad, so, regarding your predicament I know less than everyone else in the country. Would you like me to come down? Do you need any help? I am negligent by nature, you must not help me to be more so. You must write or telephone and tell me what is happening. Don't think you would be interrupting anything. Life here has not really taken off for me yet. It's nothing to do with your problems, I promise. I have always had a tendency to withdraw into myself in strange situations. It's my own fault; people are much warmer here than I am used to, and – to my shame – I can't help being a little suspicious of such friendliness. Yesterday I met someone in the street who remembered me from somewhere a long time ago. I didn't know who she was, and wasn't sure I liked her very much anyway. However, she couldn't have been friendlier and pressed me to come to a party she was giving that night. After she'd gone I threw her address in the gutter, reflecting as I did so that they are right who call it the cold, mean, inhospitable South.

I wish you would confide in me. My difficulties in adjusting to life up here have nothing to do with your breakup. I have always hidden from you what an awkward, solitary person I am, and now, five hundred miles away, you find it out! Coming here has made me very aware of my inadequacies, and, if anything, rather than complicate things, your breakup has stimulated me to do something about this. I mean I feel entirely on my own now, which can only be a good thing.

Mary is a little anxious for me, but discreet. She says in this sweet stern way each evening she sees me that I should be out of the house by now! Her mother came to stay the other day, a rich, stuffy old bag from Oxford. It was extraordinary how two people who resembled each other so closely could be so different. Mary was the spit of her, but her versions of those traits which in the mother were insensitive and unkind, in the daughter were sweet, delicate and thoughtful. Where the mother was contented and spiteful, Mary by comparison showed herself to be unhappy and compassionate. It made me think unhappiness must be the only virtue left in our world.

29th September

Dear M,

I assure you everything is fine. I am not in the least depressed. I am learning to appreciate the liveliness and the warmth. There is a bar I visit sometimes, drawn there by a slight friend. It is down a steep street off the Royal Mile, down towards the intestines of the old city. It is close and jolly in there, and I can bear it happily. The drinkers sit around rattling off their stories, smiling and laughing. I feel very stupid to admit it, but I really didn't know bars could be friendly like this. It gives me the sensation somehow of having gone back in time. There is an openness and frankness, a free way of talking and associating that I thought was long gone from the world. It is a great contrast to the bars I know in London, where the atmosphere is edgy and sharp, and people bunch up in tight little groups. The people I have got to know in the bar are kind to me. I would have thought they would interpret my quietness against me, particularly as I am so English, but they do not mind me and compliment me instead on being so serious and grave!

7th October

Dear M,

Tell me how you are. That I haven't heard from you for a while I take to be good. Why? Because I am in good spirits! The weather here is highly changeable, and that is exciting in itself. Yesterday it could not have been more threatening; as I walked home the clouds were racing above the rooftops with incredible speed.

I am sure you can imagine it: clouds swirling in like a tide above the streets. The scuttling crowds, the shop fronts in which electric lights shine down, Edinburgh fashion, on a modest selection of goods. A huge storm looked sure to burst any moment. The crowds pressed their coats to their middles and tilted into the wind; one or two countrymen walked proudly and slowly apart in the gutters.

I felt strangely out of it. Away from the shops there was no light at all, and the city's guttering depths had grown so dark and my eyes so accustomed to it that once, looking up, I caught sight of the sky through some piece of grating, and that sky, though I would expect it to be the greyest sky in the world, appeared marvellously bright and colourful. I found myself yearning towards this patch of deep strong colour as one believes one might have stretched one's heart towards the stained glass of a medieval cathedral in the middle of an interminable sermon. I found myself in love with this patch of the sombre Edinburgh heaven for its brightness and the richness of its purple. I stood and looked and became hypnotised by the conundrum that this sky, the author of the surrounding gloom which had overwhelmed the entire city, had a beauty and a power that was completely unobserved by everyone except myself.

I continued thinking this as I walked along, fighting off the universal dejection in my own way. As I strode through the gloom I kept burnishing the memory of that first vision of the bright sky piled like sacking above the city, when, for some reason, the solace of this thought suddenly failed me and, like everyone else I suppose, I went home, and drew my curtains against the day, even though it was not yet three o'clock, and lay down on my bed not expecting to see a glimpse of the sun for many weeks and months.

But then, this morning, a powerful beam of sharp light assaulted me in my bed. I woke deliciously cold and hungry. I threw off my bedclothes and stood naked by the window, surrounded by the fresh eddies of the light gusts blowing through the cracks in the casement. I showered quickly and breakfasted downstairs with Mary and Effie. Each morning we have coffee and toast and marmalade

– everything cheap as it can possibly be so as to make one moment of the day into a socialist ritual – but today such were my good spirits the occasion just felt like another charming piece of Morningside self-mortification, strangely light and easy to digest. I surprised Mary by wearing a beautiful new shirt, white and very crisp, which in turn had surprised me in my drawer. I felt clean and lively, ran down the road, thanking the sun, thanking the blue sky, thanking the cold sea air for what felt like a crude personal visitation.

Ah, it is strange, how often I have felt blessed. I do not understand why others do not confess to similar feelings themselves. Do you have this, this sudden opening up to sensations of deep joy and blessedness? Is this the foundation of your religious sensibility? I can't count the times – my head goes awry when I think specifically of this subject – but I reckon a couple of times every month I feel rich in spiritual consciousness. An intense eagerness for beauty that bears awkwardly on my schoolboy manners, a sudden power of knowledge and authority that is in utter contrast to my general insistence on my own *naïveté* and immaturity. The formalised modesty and self-deprecation which is the mark of my class is suddenly undone from within by a very pure and very licentious love of the self and all its senses. I emerge from the reverie of my solitude hit by the sense of the world, astonished by the unappreciated qualities which surround me – the beauty, the unobserved beauty! And I find I have a heart that was made to love these things. But this discovery is always a shock.

Sometimes I wonder if I am not being born afresh. Childhood was my age of cynicism and conceit and these new sensations that spring upon me are a sign of my new birth. Whatever, it is certain I have arrived at adulthood almost deprived of any experience of inspiration. And now I am assaulted by a whole number of sensations and thoughts that might have occurred to me in childhood, but which did not.

Like many others too young I persuaded myself of the degeneracy of everything so as to stain my stupid innocence. It was my habit to convict many institutions of which I had no experience of rank corruption. I suppressed my critical faculties by appearing to exercise them. In truth, the fantasies of my childhood were doctrinaire; nor do I think this was unusual. I remember, when quite young, regretting my political sense was not more developed, in the same way a Victorian child might wish it had a more beatific soul. But now I look at familiar things and see a whole world with fresh and innocent eyes. I have always wondered how delicious milk would taste if we were to drink it for the first time as adults – how amazed we would be with its smoothness, its lustrousness, its fulsomeness. These feelings which come upon me are like milk I have never tasted before . . .! My lethargy here, or rather my unhappiness here, is very much the fruit of my childish laziness, my reliance on others for everything, my complete lack of self-sufficiency. And this sudden injection of vitality into my thoughts, well, that is not so much the intrusion of the real world, it is the intrusion of my real self . . .

Anyhow, more of that later. There I was skipping down the road wondering when the high spirits would subside. Well, soon I was no longer skipping but walking, then I was standing at the bus stop in a queue. Then I was paying my money and finding my seat on the top deck. Still I felt very good. I got to my stop at the top of the Mound in the centre of town and got down from the bus with a deep determination to enjoy my life to the full. I stood on the pavement and looked around me. From this spot the gorges of the streets cut away to distant country in every direction. I turned around, admiring and comparing the different atmospheres at each point of the compass. After a while it struck me that the sunlight was brighter and the air clearer in one direction. Especially enchanted seemed to be a stretch of meadowland way the other side of the Forth estuary, which had never before looked so warm or alluring or so near. It was beautiful and I studied it with that bashful curiosity one has when one realises that a favourite picture has details of which one was previously entirely oblivious.

The wish to walk towards this sunny country came upon me as I was on the step of a café I have taken to visiting. I was still thinking about walking there as I stepped through the door. 'Why would I want to walk to the outskirts of the city?' I asked myself. 'This is a strange proposition to make to yourself.' As I came in, the grandmother who works there saw I was in a quandary, and asked me what was on my mind. I told her that I suddenly wanted to go to the sea. 'Leave your bag of books here,' she said, 'and go.' If she hadn't told me, I would not have gone. As I was bending down to put the bag behind the counter, she said something sweet like, 'Take advantage of your youth, son.' I set off, blithe and excited. Soon I was picking my way down the steep Edinburgh pavements towards the Firth. Soon I had broached the borders of my knowledge and was in new territory, beyond the province of maintained gentility, and into an area of bolder decay. Here self-sufficiency had faded in the same way that grandeur fades, leaving an intact ghost to preside over restricted lives. The streets flattened out and grew dirtier, the shops smaller and more interesting. In the streets almost everyone seemed to be carrying bags of one sort or another; their bags gave them the look of never having gone anywhere else.

I will never go there again, past the grocers' shops, smelling the sea, feeling on my fingertips and in my palms that brand of Scotch contentment that hangs just above desperation. And it makes us aware of the intensity of our perceptions to go to a place knowing that we will never go there again. I took a long time over my walk, enjoying every moment of it. Eventually I came up to a whitewashed concrete wall at the side of a shop, against which the Firth washed. There were bins, seagulls and across the grey water the band of country which looked so alluring from the Mound. There was no way across, nor was there any way I could have been disappointed. I peered over the concrete wall a while, and then I turned around and began to walk back. I suppose because it was a journey which none would envy I was pleased with myself at having made it. Every moment of the five or so hours it took me felt important and unusual. I thought of the grandmother in the café sending me on my way, and how, if she asked me, I would describe my enjoyment of my trip. Even as I was walking along I had no doubt that this day would join that tiny band of memories that return often, unprompted and un-understood. Why did I make a holy quest from so unenterprising an outing? I hesitate to answer. I can only think of this journey as a sort of pilgrimage because the faith which it honours is shared by none beside myself. The piquancy of the occasion was the complete solitude in which I turned these thoughts. And this is the shape I have given my life; my will is like an inward alchemy, turning what is bleak and grey into a gold I can discover everywhere.

16th October

Dear Paul,

I am pursued by coincidence. Last week I noticed a man who in gesture and in manner resembled xxxx. I found this very interesting, and watched him for half an hour as he consulted various books in the library. I considered going up to him and talking to him, but he had so clearly that awkwardness and diffidence that makes friendship with xxxx so difficult and complicated that I just watched him from a distance, smiling at the growing band of similarities. After a while, getting nothing done myself, I packed up and left the library, but wherever I went I saw him. Many times he looked directly at me, and didn't seem to notice me. Either this or he was blankly calculating the mounting improbability of it all. Four times in one day, and in four different places, we came within touching distance of one another. He wasn't following me and I certainly wasn't following him.

That we visited identical places suggested we had tastes in common. I couldn't help but think that fate was driving us together and wanted us to know each other. And was going to extraordinary lengths because we refused to acknowledge each other. Eventually I returned to the library, planning to concentrate on my work if I did not have the heart to confront this man. I was able to spend several hours over my books without looking up once, but, as I was leaving, I found him leaving also. By some absurd chance we were both heading for the same automatic barrier, and even more absurdly we both tried to go through it at the same time. We got stuck! It was too much. He was so flustered that I couldn't doubt any longer that he had been aware of me. I laughed, impressed by the lengths to which fate had gone to jam us together. We couldn't avoid each other now. We exchanged our first words: I apologised, he said something I did not catch. I told him my name and then asked him if he would like to come and have a drink. He looked as surprised as if I had propositioned him, and walked off fast, blushing and waving his hand as if some insect that had been pestering him had finally tried to sting him. Ah! what a mistake I had made. Immediately I saw he was nothing like our friend xxxx. For all the outward resemblance, he had not that fine, slow, gracious mind which takes in everything quicker than an eye can wink. If he had had anything in common with xxxx, at the very least he would have smiled at the comedy of my confusion!

At home I spent my evening remembering how I first met xxxx. You told me to talk to him, you told me that he was an extraordinary person. I did as you said. I went up to him where he sat in his familiar isolation and silence and spoke to him, and he looked up at me and smiled and replied, and the articulate majesty of his reply and the beauty of his smile quite overwhelmed me, and for many days afterward I was supported on a cloud of happiness, which was very like how I imagined love must feel . . .

I miss you, Paul, I need your sure sense to guide me to someone I can talk with!

7th November

Dear M,

In a deeply emphatic way Edinburgh crystallises the social divisions between north and south, Scottish and English, rich and poor, proud and meek, intense and frivolous. The English who come to the university here are almost all well-born and flagrantly snobbish. I do not know why it should be, but I have never met idiocy paraded with such open self-satisfaction before. Their voices are plummy, and they use them loudly, enjoying the bad impression their assumption of superiority spreads amongst the keen, sensitive Scots. I, to my great discomfort, have all the attributes of the insensitive. I am tall, I wear a big coat and I have my English accent. There is no open hostility, but there is enough resentment to add an extra burden to the awkwardness I already feel. It counts for nothing of course that I deplore the barbarity of my kind. My better parts have no outlet and might as well not exist. I have not found a soul-mate to reassure me that I am no different from these insensitive, snobbish oafs.

I look upon Edinburgh student life as a paradigm of our world and all its wretched divisions of class, wealth, race, age, sex. For many of these students, this is the last time in their lives that they will cast themselves into an unknown sea and, though it is not surprising that they stick, at first, entirely to their own kind, they soon establish their complacency and their limitations. They will never be exposed to uncertainty again, they are at their strongest and their most adventurous, and they have responded timidly. The self-enclosing social apartheid of the young students buries their chances of finding real happiness. They are not aware of their utter conventionality.

I have been thinking a lot about how children make themselves dishonest. In the nursery we learn to misrepresent ourselves to everyone except our close friends. (It's not that we don't lie to our close friends, it's just that they know us well enough to see through our lies.) This dishonesty becomes so ingrained that it ceases to trouble our conscience. I realise now that I have never been an honest person, I remember how I have always lied about things, to myself, and about myself. I know I have never met an honest person my own age.

And for some reason I have been thinking about how honesty must be recovered if we wish to find any real happiness in this world. My feeling is that the reason so many of us find this world boring and enervating is due first to the false and dishonest idea we keep about ourselves. We refuse to find anything interesting, we refuse to find anything original unless it panders to our cynicism.

I doubt I would have discovered these feelings elsewhere; for not only is Edinburgh student society possibly the most rigidly stratified since pre-revolutionary France, but I have the feeling that the city outside the university harbours the antithesis of this corruption. Daily you see walking in the street people who have the look of being able to bridge these divisions and confound these constraints. A look which strikes you as a mark of honesty first, and a mark of power second. You tell these people from the way they walk and the way they talk. This sounds unlikely, and perhaps even crazily deluded and optimistic, but I am convinced these people exist, and having nothing better to do, I will now seek them out until I have satisfied myself that I am right. There are many Scots who really haven't compromised with the modern world, whose attitude is that a man is a man and that is that. I believe it is an old Scottish virtue that Robbie Burns was said to epitomise, being as good and forceful a talker with duchesses as with ostlers. An anachronistic virtue, you might think, but still palpable!

If this letter strikes you as heavily worked over, it is! I hope you are not bored by it, but I have been very preoccupied with these things, and needed to sort my thoughts out, and as I wanted to write to you I did both at the same time.

All my love, XXX

P.S. By the way, these are my own thoughts. I am sure they are not original, but one reason for writing them to you was to avoid the indignity of a friend accusing me of paraphrasing some sociologist for my own conceit!

14th November

Dear Paul,

I did as you suggested and joined the student Labour Party. I don't know how regular a member I shall become. There can be few more censorious and earnest people than my comrades, and no people in all the world less disposed to welcome someone like myself. The only kindness they have shown me so far was in accepting my money in exchange for a membership card. The business of my joining up was the most unsmiling forty-five minutes I have ever spent. They disdain even to disapprove of me. I am suffered at their meetings but I cannot think how they would react if I were to open my mouth. They are anti-libertarian Calvinists, all the more daunting and unforgiving because they feel themselves surrounded by licentious reprobates with English accents. I have made one friend among them, however, not at the meetings, we recognised each other elsewhere. He is called Ian and he comes from Paisley. He is gentle and quiet, brought up a Trotskyist to think of little else but revolution, is the first member of his family to go to university and is expected to return to Paisley and become a leading light in the revolutionary movement. He is suspiciously fond of non-political literature, however. We meet and talk about books together with what seems to be a subversive animation, and he has read a great deal. He is much more serious than I and sometimes our conversations grow boring; other times, we go to see films together. I like him, but I do not think of him when we are not together. The cord of loneliness which attaches us is not very strong.

The student Labour Party is a disappointment. There is something indescribably futile in the formalised seriousness of this group of young people. Individually they are sincere, collectively ridiculous. I wonder if we have not all spent our childhood so superficially that we now play at maturity.

Still I am not sure I don't prefer being with them than with the noisy, conceited, cocktail-party-giving, monocle-wearing English student twits. There could be no greater contrast between the bursting inconsequentiality of the boisterous English and the constrained earnestness of this politically demonstrative Ian. And I find myself in every and in no camp. Daily I make myself ridiculous by expressing ideas I do not believe in or suppressing feelings which I do. Dear Paul, I am grateful that we are separated, that we cannot watch each other posture and pose ourselves into the ridiculous shapes we are bound to become.

14th November

Dear M,

Thanks for your last letter. These thoughts are still preoccupying me. And I still mean to find the honesty that stalks these streets, and exert my own innocence. With luck, if I am sincere about being honest I will grow brave.

Being alone so much one hopes for all sorts of things . . .

P.S. I am very sorry about the news. I wish this had not happened.

1st December

Dear Paul,

I had an adventure of sorts the other night. Let me tell you about it. I went to see a film, and when I came out I found that several inches of snow had fallen. I wanted to walk home, though it was about two or three miles, and already several degrees below freezing. When I got back I couldn't find my key. The lights were out, and though I knew that Mary or Tom wouldn't have minded in the least being woken up, I couldn't bring myself to bang on the door. I had a thick coat on, and I had some warm trousers in a bag in the garage which I put over my jeans, and I thought I would stay out through the night. I walked around. I have made one, very slight friend here, and I went to the part of town where I knew she lived. She had given me her address but I couldn't remember either the street name or the number of the flat. She had told me roughly where to find it, and I hoped that if I looked I might find her. She is very friendly and distinctive. I thought I would immediately be able to tell just which window was hers if only I could find the right street. So I wandered through the town, street after street, examining all the names and racking my brains. Of course I was having a lovely time. A very strong moon was out, shining down on the streets like a policeman's torch. I spent several hours roaming, and one by one the lights in the windows went out.

We have never talked about it, I have never asked if you, like me, spend lonely hours walking through the streets at night. I used to think that through a window I might find my way to sex, but of course this quest became a survey of human mortification. I now no longer know my motive for looking into every lit-up room. Is it to see a voluptuous naked woman beckoning me, or is it to see desolation exposed? So often I spend the night hours searching out lights in houses and in flats, longing to see some sign of human warmth, and not once have I been shown the barest gesture of kindness through a window at night. Only cold indifference. The city is a desert of love I think. The tragedy of our existence would not be so invisible were its beauties not so forlornly displayed. It would today require a supreme artist even to feel, much less to represent, the wonders of our life.

Anyhow, dear Paul, to return to my adventure. Edinburgh revealed little. I spent the night walking the streets to keep warm. I was in a daze for most of the time. Eventually, after a long time, morning came around. I heard the sound of horses' hooves drawing the milkcarts over the cobblestones. The streets became busier. From my friend's quarter I headed off towards my house, reckoning Mary would soon be up, and I went by way of the Grassmarket, a sunken part of the old town. There, floundering through the snow, I met a tramp who stopped me for the price of a cup of tea. As I fumbled in my pockets he saw how cold I was, put his hand on my shoulder and said he would take me back to his hostel and warm me up. Numb and exhausted I walked by his side the few steps to the door and was taken in and sat down on a bench beside five or six old men. I told them of my night. I think I must have spoken at length. I was aware in my relief of speaking more than I had spoken in all the weeks of my stay in this city. To the tale of my night's hardships they listened with sweet and inappropriate indulgence, and I found myself, almost for the first time in my life I think, fallen among friends. One old man, called Terence, I took to especially. He has that nervous manner of clever men of laughing at everything he says, and looking gravely at everything that is said to him. He nods his head continually and wipes back from his forehead with his hand a very elegant thin hank of grey hair. He has a fine saloon bar manner, which usually has him sitting crosswise on the bench with one one leg crossed over the other, fidgeting and smoking, chuckling, giving out quotes from Shakespeare, Burns and Hancock. He was surprised I, a Sassenach, had read or cared for Burns. I proved to him that my enthusiasm was genuine when I told him that 'Love and Liberty' was my favourite; he whipped off the first stanza with an extraordinary explosion of grace and ability, and disappointed us all by refusing to give any more. We shouted and we cheered, we stamped our feet and cried. Terence relented and recited it all. Amazingly, though it lasts for thirty or forty minutes, none of us doubted he had it all in his head ready for delivery. I mean we none of us thought we were asking him to do anything difficult. He gave it to us and how!

Here, because I know you don't know it, and you cannot fail to enjoy it, is the first part.

When lyart leaves bestrow the yird . . .

In English, 'when grey leaves cover the earth . . .' Is not that a good beginning? What else has ever given you such a strong reminder of that feeling of autumn, when the grey light of the morning seems to be falling as soon as you open your eyes, and the wet grey leaves pasted over the earth grow pale in the falling gloom? (You've had enough of the English for now, you've got the picture.)

> *When lyart leaves bestrow the yird,*
> *Or wavering like the bauckie-bird,*
>   *Bedim cauld Boreas' blast;*
> *When hailstanes drive wi' bitter skyte,*
> *And infant frosts begin to bite,*
>   *In hoary cranreuch drest;*

Ae night at e'en a merry core
    O' randie, gangrel bodies,
In Poosie-Nansie's held the splore,
    To drink their orra duddies;
        Wi' quaffing an' laughing,
            They ranted an' they sang,
        Wi' jumping an' thumping,
            The vera girdle rang.

First, neist the fire, in auld red rags,
Ane sat, weel brac'd wi' mealy bags,
    And knapsack a' in order;
His doxy lay within his arm;
Wi usquebae an' blankets warm
    She blinkit on her sodger;
An' aye he gies the tozie drab
    The tither skelpin kiss,
While she held up her greedy gab,
    Just like an aumous dish;
        Ilk smack still did crack still,
            Just like a cadger's whip;
        Then staggerin an' swaggering
            He roar'd this ditty up—

(And this air is sung to the tune of 'I was a Sodger
Laddie')

I am a son of Mars who have been in many wars,
    And show my cuts and scars wherever I come;

—— 41 ——

This here was for a wench, and that other in a trench,
When welcoming the French at the sound of the
  drum . . .

Even if you don't like like it on first viewing,
believe me it is good, very, very good! And there's
much more. The scene was like that described in
the poem: the bums sitting round the benches
against the wall, and Terence, sweating, whipping
back his hank of hair, lollopping about the room,
half like a bandage-footed old Glasgow bum, half
like a fop from a drawing-room engraving of the
eighteenth century; you know, thin, washed-out
colours, the exaggerated flounces of a tired old
body, still animated and excited . . . He performed
each of the songs in his whippy old voice, suggest-
ing the tune, twirling his finger around in the air
to fill out the inadequacies. It was the most sublime
and erratic performance I have ever seen, full of
character, full of the knowledge of life. All the old
figures in Burns' great low-life epic Terence had
met, from the war veteran to the midget fiddler to
the last great hero, the strong-minded, clear-
headed, soliloquising shy republican bum who
shouts out to the uproarious approval of his
drunken audience:

What is title, what is treasure,
  What is reputation's care?

If we lead a life of pleasure,
  'Tis no matter how or where!

A fig for those by law protected!
  Liberty's a glorious feast!
Courts for cowards were erected,
  Churches built to please the priest.

Life is all a variorum,
  We regard not how it goes,
Let them cant about decorum
  Who have character to lose . . .

He was busy giving us this for some thirty minutes, without a break. He sat down when it was over. We whooped him in our own way, celebrated him unstintingly. None knew the cause of this great oration, this unexpected feat. I tell you Olivier would have been open-mouthed with jealous wonder, Charles Laughton would have dumbly bowed.

I admired his performance so much, I was ecstatic and could not find breath enough for all the ways I had to praise it, and yet once the topic of our conversation turned to myself my words began to falter. Though his manner was discreet and his whole demeanour flopped down several gears to take account of my shyness I realised that I was bound to be a genuine source of perplexity.

These men were interested in me and there was nothing I could find to say about myself to interest them. I had led a life of privilege and carelessness, my observations and experiences were, for them, of the most inconsequential kind. We were thoroughly well disposed to one another, we had a bond, and yet I was very weak stuff to be attached to. This was not wholly my fault of course, but my old feelings of irrepressible inadequacy flooded over me and made me so sad I was not more resourceful that when Terence asked me if I had a girl, I lied and said yes. I told him I was in love with the finest girl in the world. Oh, it would make your eyes water to see how this affected everyone, how my queer and unspeakable awkwardness was suddenly redeemed. Ah my! How the topic of sex cheered everyone up! He asked me who the girl was, and I told him about the one friend I mentioned earlier in the letter – whose flat I had been looking for. He asked her name, and for a description of her, and after listening to me with his head cocked on one side even more cutely than he usually holds it, then most extraordinarily he declared he loved her too, not in the same way that I did, he winked, but he loved her. I had not expected this, but it was quite true that Terence and this girl were old friends. They had known each other, he said, a good few months, drank together in the same bar. He spoke very vividly of her and described her for everyone so fully that I could not doubt he was talking about the girl I had lied and said I loved. Oh Terence Rigby you are a wonderful man. Though my lie would be revealed I echoed his whoops and smiled till my face hurt when he slapped his thigh.

Then he began again, this bum-philosopher, alight with pleasure, beating off on a glowing disquisition about the enormous joy coincidence brings to every bum life; telling me – the only one there who didn't know – how it was the best thing in all the world to run into someone and discover that you 'shared a pal, or a girl, even if it was all long ago . . .' Grinning and winking around at us all, he cried, he re-enacted the joy of such moments. Four or five little vignettes flashed by, all of which told such vivid stories from his life, I barely caught the substance of two of them, the winter's day in Stirling, in the bus station, when miraculously appeared 'the wee chap from Mandalay', as Terence called him. Or the morning at the port, when from way out he saw his old tinker friend standing by the rail of the approaching boat. He was transported back to each of these occasions and after spinning round he announced to us all so distinctly that I can remember his very words: 'You whoop at the wonder of it. The intoxication is powerful, and lasts in the memory for a long time as a consolation for the hardships and the uncertainty and unhappiness of life. These chance meetings, these coincidences, make the stars shine bright. They persuade you that you have not been forgotten in the world. That you are not so deeply pressed down in oblivion that chance cannot sometime smile on you.' I felt all this, admired all this, careless that of this miraculous joy I was a false harbinger.

He is a beautiful man, he has lived. He expresses the opinions of experience, and these opinions have in them that lovely warmth and generosity that a person can spread around themselves having over-come many obstacles and many hard places. His smile seems to suggest we could all be free, if we had the stamina of this man. Freedom, I think, exists mostly today in the past tense, and if it has been, will announce itself as a sort of exhaustion. Until I met him I realised I had never met an admirable man or woman in my life. This was a surprise. I had read about people admiring other people, and I had met envied people and people who thought them-selves enviable, but I had never admired anyone for the way they lived, for the way they did themselves good by being free and generous. Am I being repet-itive over this? I seem to repeat the same words, in the same order, again and again! But do you agree? Until I met Terence I did not realise that you could read so quickly or so much of the essential details of a person's character, and the essential decisions they have made in their life. And I did not know this because I had never met someone before in whom these details and decisions were so wholly admirable. It is a strange confession, but until I met Terence, and liked him so immensely and so immediately, I didn't realise how penetrating we are, how quickly we can gather all we might ever need to know about a person . . .

13th January

Dear M,

You ask about my friends . . . There would be more to tell you if . . . if I had not started to be particularly taken with one . . .

I have begun to make friends, very loose friends, with a girl who I consider remarkable. It is unlikely we shall ever become close, for we are very unalike. Yet it is this difference between us, this dissimilarity in our lives, that makes our friendship, at present, strong. It sounds, I am sure, like I am a little in love with her, and perhaps I am, for I have never met someone I find so fascinating, and who steals all interest from everyone else about me.

She is so animated, so full of positive qualities that I cannot describe her without seeming to be infatuated with her. Yet she gives me no reason to be abashed, she is always pleased to see everyone, and though I see she calculates exactly what goes on inside people's heads, she gives no indication of doing so. It is not that she pretends to be dumb, but she does not pretend to be clever, and so almost everyone fails to credit her brilliance. I think I am the only person who realises the penetration of her intuition. She sees into everyone and judges them very crisply, but with great generosity. She is a paragon of understanding, she will become a remarkable woman, as an idea I am completely besotted by her. She gives me no reason to be afraid of her. There is no one kinder or more generous. She is beautiful in a way I have never believed I could feel someone to be beautiful . . . Her beauty is fascinating, captivating beyond . . . thought or appreciation! I have never admired anyone before. She is exotic but counts herself ordinary; is amazingly sharp and quick-witted, she alternates between the most patient kindness and the most abrupt rudeness on the justice of an instant . . . She makes me laugh until I cry. She is friendly and open, she has a million friends, she is delighted to see everyone. People flock to her. She is entirely unsuspicious and fearless of friendships or other people. It is very easy and happy to be with her. Of course, I am now neglecting my work, but my education has begun at last. Now I am learning something about the world. She is brilliant, she teaches me countless new pleasures to be found in being alive. There is no more attractive thought in all the world than the thought of being intimate with her, or in her thoughts, or able to speak deeply with her.

She was born on a farm in Sussex where her family still live. She is the youngest of many brothers and sisters. Her father died last year, he was old, was born in fact before the First World War. His memory is very tender for her and she confesses a great fear that she never expressed all the love she felt for him while he was alive. Her mother, who remains alone in the farm on the hill, is difficult and demanding, and she, being the youngest of the children, is often called down to be with her. She does this willingly, though she is so far away. She is often away, and this explains why I seldom see her in the class where I met her; my attendance, conversely, is very good. But I do not listen to the lectures, I berate myself for not having written down all the extraordinary things she has already said that I have forgotten!

I hope you are well. I love you very much. And now, let me say goodbye.

midnight, or very late, in my room

17th January

Dear Paul,

This morning, walking down in the Grass-market, I heard a tune whistled that haunted me. I seemed to know it already and so could memorise it, and later I came across Terence. I was looking for him, and I found him. The song was still in my memory, and I asked him if he knew it. I whistled it to him and Terence then supplied me with the words. It goes like this:

Come all you tramps and hawkers
ye gatherers of lore.
That tramps the country round and round,
come listen one and all.
I'll tell to you a movin' tale
of sights that I have seen.
It's far into the snowy north
and south by Gretna Green.
Of't times I've laughed unto myself
while trudging on the road
wi my bag of blow upon my back
my face as brown's a toad
wi' lamps and cakes and tattie scones
cheese and bracksie ham

> *It's no thinking whar I'm coming frae*
> *nor whar I'm going to gan.*

It is quite extraordinarily exquisite, and when sung by an old Scottish tramp, it is like a new colour was given its musical equivalent. The rapture opens unbearably wide in the last verse:

> *But I'm happy in the summertime*
> *beneath the bright blue sky*
> *nae thinking in the morning*
> *whar I do lie . . .*

And closes in a forlorn postscript:

> *and if the weather does permit*
> *I'm happy every day . . .*

The song is such a strange mixture of lament and rhapsody. The tune was familiar; I questioned Terence about it, and told him that it reminded me of a Dylan song. Clever old Terence knew that this was one of a series of begging songs recorded in the fifties by Ewan MacColl. Robert Dylan, as Terence called him, was interested in these songs, and incorporated some of the melodies into his own ballads of that time, circa *John Wesley Harding*.

I don't know why, but this great tramp tradition lies very much beneath the surface of Scotland.

The whole country is continually celebrating itself, and yet these songs, which are the most evocative folk songs in the world, are poorly neglected. This is a great thing of course for preserving their feel. I wish I could give you a bit of their flavour. Or tell you the power they have when heard floating over the cold air . . .

They are the expression of a strain of independence, repeatedly checked by the world, till nothing is left but a relish for the freedom of poverty. It is as if the plangency of St Francis naked among the birds, in the rank marshes, can still be heard in the voice of Terence. Terence is not quite one of these old tramps himself. He is a man broken through drink and family sadnesses, but his voice, when he tells his stories, or sings his songs, becomes the voice of men who were not broken or ruined, but who lived with a slow, simple seriousness that encountered poverty, misery, the cruelty of landlords, and found consolation in all the natural beauties of their native Scotland. Tramping as a spiritual solace is unique to Presbyterian Scotland, where the poor are never affronted or shamed by poverty. The measured consideration in the voice, as delicate as a wistful reed, sustains itself as long as the great mountains.

Before this happened I copied out for you a letter I wrote to my mother. It is the only way I can confess something to you . . .

I have begun to make friends, very loose friends, with a girl who I consider remarkable. It is unlikely we shall ever become close, for we are very unalike. Yet it is this difference between us, this dissimilarity in our lives, that makes our friendship, at present, strong. It sounds, I am sure, like I am a little in love with her, and perhaps I am, for I have never met someone I find so fascinating, and who steals all interest from everyone else about me.

She is so animated, so full of positive qualities that I cannot describe her without seeming to be infatuated with her. Yet she gives me no reason to be abashed, she is always pleased to see everyone, and though I see she calculates exactly what goes on inside people's heads, she gives no indication of doing so. It is not that she pretends to be dumb, but she does not pretend to be clever, and so almost everyone fails to credit her brilliance. I think I am the only person who realises the penetration of her intuition. She sees into everyone and judges them very crisply, but with great generosity. She is a paragon of understanding, she will become a remarkable woman, as an idea I am completely besotted by her. She gives me no reason to be afraid of her. There is no one kinder or more generous. She is beautiful in a way I have never believed I could feel someone to be beautiful . . . Her beauty is fascinating, captivating beyond . . . thought or appreciation! I have never admired anyone before.

She is exotic but counts herself ordinary; is amazingly sharp and quick-witted, she alternates between the most patient kindness and the most abrupt rudeness on the justice of an instant. . . She makes me laugh until I cry. She is friendly and open, she has a million friends, she is delighted to see everyone. People flock to her. She is entirely unsuspicious and fearless of friendships or other people. It is very easy and happy to be with her. Of course, I am now neglecting my work, but my education has begun at last. Now I am learning something about the world. She is brilliant, she teaches me countless new pleasures to be found in being alive. There is no more attractive thought in all the world than the thought of being intimate with her, or in her thoughts, or able to speak deeply with her.

She was born on a farm in Sussex where her family still live. She is the youngest of many brothers and sisters. Her father died last year, he was old, was born in fact before the First World War. His memory is very tender for her and she confesses a great fear that she never expressed all the love she felt for him while he was alive. Her mother, who remains alone in the farm on the hill, is difficult and demanding, and she, being the youngest of the children, is often called down to be with her. She does this willingly, though she is so far away. She is often away, and this explains why I seldom see her in the class where I met her; my attendance, conversely, is very good.

But I do not listen to the lectures, I berate myself for not having written down all the extraordinary things she has already said that I have forgotten!

By the way, her name is Kate. I am sure you have guessed that this is the girl whom I told Terence and his pals was my girlfriend. It could have been awkward for me if Terence was not the most discreet man in the world. Once I bumped into Terence and Kate when they were out together. Not only did Terence not say the slightest word to embarrass me, but he did not even show me that he remembered my declaration of love for this girl. Can you conceive of such splendour?

20th February

Dear Paul,

There is nothing so good as being alone. 'If the weather does permit . . .' My heart sings!

I let coincidence rule my life, and its reliability persuades me it is my fate to be happy! All I care about now is seeing my friend Katie. But this can never be planned. Edinburgh is small enough that you regularly bump into people in the streets. Whenever I am at my sunniest, whenever I want to, I bump into Katie. The chance of these meetings suits the casual liveliness of our friendship. To have a friendship as random, as unplanned as this, suits us both. Though we always say we shall make a plan to meet, we never do, but leave each other cheerfully wondering if we shall ever see each other again.

I hope you are well. I love you very much. And now, let me say goodbye.

2nd March

Dear M,

Thanks for your note. I wouldn't agree I have a girlfriend – far from it. It is almost embarrassing to think of her in that relationship, we are so unlike each other. Our friendship consists entirely of chance meetings on the street. I have never been to her place and she has never been to mine. I don't know any of her friends and she knows none of mine. I imagine a great many men press themselves on her and she doesn't want another.

I walked into a Polish delicatessen the other day, and while I was buying some coffee I heard Kate's voice in a back room. She was being given tea by the owner, an old Polish woman who had struck me before as being unfriendly. Kate heard my voice in the shop, told the shopkeeper about me and I found myself also invited into the back room to tea – a feast of chocolate figs and shortbread and sausage sandwiches. Quite by chance I had walked into the shop where Katie does all her shopping. The conversation between her and Krisha – the proprietress – was music to listen to. No two people could be more unalike, this old stolid Polish woman, who had been through the war in Poland, lost family and two husbands, who had slowly built some semblance of security for herself by opening a shop in 1950s Edinburgh, and sticking to it, day in and day out. And yet, as I listened, the conversation between them sounded like a piece of fine music, of genuine feeling and understanding, and sympathy. Of course it was polite and formal, it could not be anything else, but despite being that it was still vital – anything but false. I did not hear Kate express one false sentiment or one untrue opinion. Many times the old Polish woman laughed and laughed at Kate's stories. It is a proper friendship, and both are aware it is unusual. I found it very remarkable. For me, it was almost a perfect occasion, like being the only person allowed to the sole performance of an exquisite film. Ah! It was so interesting, there was so much to taste and think about and wonder about, as I sat there silent in my chair. The conversation being slow and deliberate gave me so much time to turn over each phrase, each little ejaculation, in my mind. When it was all over it was like leaving a cinema or a theatre with that extra gravity and weight in your insides that only a really fine production of a really fine play can give you. I thought nothing about this old woman before, and now I was astonished at how much she interested me – interest which I would never have discovered for myself. Katie has such an intuitive compass of perception that the shades of personality of this weary, slow old woman were suddenly as easy to read, and as brilliantly lit up, as

in a three-year-old child. The genius of this friendship was Kate's; Krisha acknowledged this to me in
the way she smiled a farewell to me before direct-
ing her eyes in almost awelike reverence at the back
of Katie – done entirely for my benefit, to show
me how highly she thought of my friend. As we
walked away Katie continued to talk about Krisha,
and to unveil to me more about her, and to further
emphasise what an extraordinary person she was;
though I was drawn deep into Krisha's life, I did
not stop thinking that I had never seen someone so
young so interest someone so old.

My tea with the old Polish woman showed me
that nothing is richer or more fascinating than those
regions towards which self-interest and self-satisfaction will never lead us.

4th March

Dear Paul,

No, it doesn't seem in the least likely that this person could ever be my girlfriend. She is far too grown-up, too sophisticated, too rich in spirit, too diverse in tastes to find a faltering, dejected boy like myself attractive. My wish for a girlfriend – which was never very strong in the first place – is now blasted into that bin of childish dreams, where it takes up no more space than the dream of wanting to be a racing driver. It now seems absurd, the thought of wanting to attach yourself to someone as young and limited as yourself. To join erotic intentions with the fumbling attempt at self-domestication. I look around at people my own age as they hitch themselves together. To each other I know they expose something of their sensitive beings, that they live freshly and excitedly with each other, but it is also true that thus satisfied they set aside the remainder of the world, at one remove from their keenest interest, and fail to think or see how other people feel or live at all. And anything which makes you less observant, less interested a participant in the general, random, self-dissipating facts of universal existence, is to be avoided. Why live, if not to acquire more of a feel for the sharp, raw edges of the world? This is my motto now.

Today the rain had been falling in a light mist all morning. Too bored for work of any kind, and too dejected for another disgusting lunch in the canteen, I began to walk home, across the Meadows, which were sloppy with mud and mire, over my bootsides even. Picture me stolidly keeping my way across the slippery park, thinking purposeful thoughts. And then I slipped and fell and as I sprawled in the mud I was more ludicrous to myself than ever before. No one else was there, no one else would have crossed that pathless place, but me. The absence of any witnesses to my idiocy only increased my embarrassment.

There are no accidents. Attempting to steel my head with all sorts of pointed meditations I ended up splashing around in a mudbath, which showed, I thought, the extent of my misgivings for my childishness.

20th March

Dear M,

Yes, I would like to tell you more about Katie! She knew about our family unhappiness from the papers; I told her all about it, and you. I told her that Dad had been unfaithful to you before, that he always seemed to come back, and that you still loved him. She expressed great sympathy for you, and from my description she said she believed you must be a wonderful woman. She said I was very lucky to have such a mother. She is the one person who I have ever talked about this with who had no curiosity to know what Dad's famous girlfriend was actually like. She didn't ask about her once, which is a fantastic thing. People generally like to have their sympathy repaid with a tittle of gossip, and though I expect it now, whenever anyone asks me about it all I am sickened. I then asked Kate about her home.

She is the youngest of a family of five, three brothers and one sister; a few months ago their father died. She loved him enormously, and she described to me a wonderful man. His death was quite miserable. It is an awful story. It had been a close but stormy marriage between him and Kate's mother. Her father, said Kate, was the most peaceable and gentle of men, but his life had been much bothered by the frequent bad tempers of his wife. About six months ago he fell ill, and though he was old – in his mid-seventies – it was not serious. Kate's mother was secretly convinced however of his imminent death and became so distraught at the prospect of being left alone by her husband that she began behaving with the utmost strangeness to her children. She refused to acknowledge his worsening condition, made it very difficult for the children to be near him and encouraged them to stay away from home, so that as he began to sink he was neglected. He died in an empty hospital bedroom, with none of his five children beside him, to hold his hand or show him any affection. He had been so kind to them, and they all loved him and venerated him so much that the thought of his solitary death destroyed them completely. Kate learnt that he died while she had been in a nightclub in London, the worst possible place of all. Since that moment she has been tormented by the awful fact that she and her brothers and sister left their father at the time of his greatest need of them; none of them thinking of the consequences of such an abandonment for him, or for themselves. I have never heard misgivings expressed with such pain as when she told me about his lonely death.

This awful story makes her present ebullience, her liveliness, her good humour seem almost incredible. I tried to ask her about this, about how, or why, she maintained such an appearance of happiness when her heart had been so wounded. But I couldn't really probe like this without seeming to question her sincerity. I don't know if it's possible that I have described her in any way to do her justice but there is no one whose manner and whose spirit is less artificial or contrived.

I met her a few days after this going into a phone box. She said she had to call her mother, and afterwards we could go and have a drink. I waited outside and listened to the conversation. There was no trace of coldness or resentment. I listened to her for twenty minutes cheering her mother on the phone. She could not have been kinder or more considerate. She came out of the phone box and said she couldn't come with me because she had to catch the next train down south. She had heard, she said, in her mother's voice, a need for her to return. 'Did she say as much?' I asked. 'No,' she said, but something made her feel she ought to go. I asked unkindly − because I didn't think the mother deserved such consideration − what would be the result if she didn't go, but she said she couldn't answer that, she didn't know that. It was awkward to question her about it because she really didn't know, and was responding to an instinct only. I gained the impression that she had made a vow to herself on hearing of her father's death never to put her own interest before someone to whom she owed any obligation. Her dutifulness to her mother is the mark of extraordinary disinterestedness. She does not know this, I think, nor does anyone else.

I saw her three days later. Her mother, she said, was very surprised she had turned up, had insisted there had been no need for her to come down. It was absolutely pointless to ask Kate if her instinct had been right. Of course it was. In some ways I feel I have met someone whose instincts are deeply connected to their conscience. This strikes me as a marvel.

28th March

Dear Paul,

I so enjoy her company that I know the feeling must be mutual. Yet still we meet only by chance, and never arrange anything. I don't want to press myself further in her life than she wishes to invite me, and much of the time I am persuaded I am no more to her than an occasional friend. But then I remember little confidences she has shown me and sharp, warm looks which I know she would not give another, and I am persuaded I have a right to hope . . .

2nd April

Dear Paul,

Term is coming to a close. The spring holidays
are upon us. I have not seen Kate for many days. I
can't bear the thought of us both leaving the one
place where I can expect to see her. Already I am
impatient for the start of the next term. It is enough
to give you an enthusiasm for work! I look forward
to seeing you, and, given that I cannot bring you
to meet this extraordinary person, I promise to find
other things to talk about than her.

20th April

Dear Paul,

I have a long letter to write you. It will take me many hours, probably days. I will keep to it till I have finished. I was recently transported to heaven, and the best way I can lower myself down to earth is to recall the visit to you. Because I have covered so much ground, forgive me if I start off a little stiffly!

I have missed seeing you in London very much, but I haven't really been able to cope with anything. I arrived back to discover a home sad and unhappy beyond anything I had expected; my father has gone for good. My mother's letters to me in Edinburgh gave me no idea how awful her recent weeks have been. The newspapers are full of his romance again now his new woman has announced she will be having a child. Her fame and glamour are so overwhelming that people continually come close to congratulating me on my fortune in having such a celebrated new stepmother. I don't dislike her, I don't blame her for the break-up of my parents' marriage, I just don't feel privileged by her arrival in our lives. My house is empty and quiet. No one comes, there is no one here but me and my mother. Every phone call seems to be from a journalist who wants to goad her into some outburst they can print.

The shock of finding my mother so unfortunate was particularly acute, as I arrived home with my head full of a very exciting journey I had made south with Kate. Quite by chance we found ourselves getting on the same train. A friend of hers called Katherine was also with us; we laughed and talked the whole journey and found out many things about each other. Kate lives near a town where my grandmother does her shopping. Maybe we would see each other one day when I was visiting my grandmother. We agreed that would be great!

Back with my mother, I felt my neglect of her. I was uncomfortable making any arrangement to go out. I felt obliged really not to leave the house, I would have felt guilty if she were to overhear me on the phone making an arrangement to see someone. It's not that she would resent it at all, but on one level it would compound her sense of abandonment. That is why I did not call you or see you. I am sorry, but I sat with her each evening, watching a bit of television, washing up supper, you know. I would get out late at night and walk around London. I found myself wondering all the time about Katie, who I do not expect to see for several weeks. I count the number of times we have been together, and realise they are very few. I think I have told you in detail about every moment we have spent with each other. As I walked through the streets I remembered every conversation we have ever had. They are like coins in an old box, I take them out in turns, finger them a while, and then put one back and choose another. I saw her much less often than I might have done. The journey together in the train was the first time in about two weeks that I had been with her. She came to few of the lectures we were enrolled in together, she was often away. She made many trips to be with her mother; also she has been going a lot to Amsterdam where she has a whole circuit of people with whom she takes huge amounts of speed.

Whenever I sit alone in the heartbroken house or wander the streets I think of her. I know at these moments she is certainly surrounded by crowds of people. My incompatibility with the girl I love could not be more stark. My mother planned a visit to friends in the Wye valley and asked me to go with her; I went instead to visit my grandmother in Sussex.

My grandmother, who has lived alone a long time, has become for me the evocation of the sadness of maturity. In my adolescence, she, more than anyone else, represented the vanishing of childhood happiness. To discover the limitations of this old woman I had loved since boyhood and to grow critical of her was one of the saddest pains of adolescence. Such an irritable, inconsequential old bird she was, and only really lovable to a young curly-headed boy like I had been. Now there is an advantage from her vague senility, and that is that she treats me again like I was eight years old. She makes us cottage pie, she asks me to run down to the village shop, and gives me a coin for a lolly. She scolds me for not getting up early enough, we play tiddlywinks together. She nods off a great deal, and now tends to talk more when she is alone than when I am with her. We sit a lot in the kitchen, she reading, or looking at her *Times*, I singing songs. I regain a strange freedom in this enforced infantilism, I remember the pleasure of being naughty, and am so. What extraordinary creatures we are! Nights I lie awake by my open window, looking over the road into Petworth Park and smoke cigarettes. The parkland is an eighteenth-century idyll, particularly at night and in the half dark of dusk and dawn. As a boy I used to jump over the wall at dusk and go for long nocturnal rambles.

On a clear night it is most beautiful. The white heathgrass, in perpetual winter roughness, catches the moonlight like snow, so that you can even see the shadows of birds as they fly down to the lake. Very still, no lights in any direction, and there is a strange contrast between the mildness and protectedness of the landscape and the sensation of remoteness. I do not know if you have been there but it is a little like Richmond Park, though finer and more dainty, and grander and more elegant. In the wind the raked lines and furrows of the long grasses are so lovely, and remind me of your description of how Van Gogh felt the grass to be screaming at him in the wind. It is at night that it is most like its original cultivated style, and returns close to the eighteenth-century ideal of wildness. It is not just that you cannot see the litterbins and the signs, the trimmings and the fences, it is that the landscape wears the glossy blackness so handsomely. My ideas as I wander through this artificial parkland, during a windy spring night, alone in this glamorous grand stage-set, is that my emotions are animated as the designers intended, as the birds wheel over the lake, as the deer start out of the brake, and strangely I am returned, whole, to a preromantic convention of wildness that is wilder, more exhilarating, than anything else I might experience today . . .

I love it too because it is so private. No one shares its loveliness with me. No one comes here at night. The only people who come in the day are National Trust types who would not dream of breaking the regulations and climbing over a wall after dark.

I know Kate lives somewhere nearby. It could be in the neighbouring village or it could be twenty miles away. I take long walks through the Sussex countryside. At every distant house I say to myself, perhaps she lives there. With her mother, and now they are together, in that room through that window at this very moment. Maybe, I say, she is thinking of me!

I think of her continually. I cannot help myself. I have come to see her as an utterly marvellous being – a unique being. Really, I swear, I would share her with anyone. It is admiration I feel for her more than desire.

I spend every minute fantasising I am with her. During my walks I talk to her as if she were with me. This is like a boyhood game. After two weeks staying with my grandmother, distracting myself in this vain way, I grow suddenly desperate. I have this opportunity to see her. She is nearby, I only need to find where. She would be pleased to see me. I feel now that I have waited so long that I have merited that fate should allow me to see her.

So, after a night spent deliberating I walk to the telephone box at six in the morning. The directory knows no number for that name. I try and remember the names of the friends she has told me about and see if I can remember where they lived. One name and one town hang together. Incredibly this produces a telephone number. Though it is just past six in the morning I phone up, I get the friend, I ask for Kate's address and phone number. I am given it, I thank the friend, I put the phone down.

Her farm is near a town about ten miles away. Automatically I step out of the phone box and set off to walk there. The sun is coming up, I am walking down country lanes past flowering May, and I start to relax. Birds are singing. The world has never looked so beautiful, its promise never more manifest or obvious than it is this morning. My heart is full of love and affection, and pure sweet country happiness. Half-man, half-boy, I take a switch as I did as a child, and switch at the hedgerows. I sing songs out loud. I keep everything but pure sensation out of my head. This is the apotheosis of my life, this swelling idyll, and waited for over years of introversion and introspection.

I knew as soon as I began that walk that I would see her and that the germ of my feelings for her would this day swell and be nourished into permanence. I knew this day was to be the most glorious of my life, that love would fix its roots and establish itself for eternity.

I did not dwell on this, in fact I put this certainty out of my head so I could feel myself surrounded by the present beauty of a spring morning. I might know that all past unhappinesses would shortly melt and that all future unhappiness should be reduced, but my chief pleasure was in the overwhelming beauty of the morning. Man, who discovers his love will live for ever, can only admire all that is beautiful in the death of a morning.

If I was oblivious of myself in admiration of the morning, it was because I knew that whatever becomes of me I shall only ever need to think of these hours and I will be grateful for my life. That long-dead morning gilded my coming love. All is dead, all is past, yet in me they live forever; that breeze, those smells, those birds singing gave such a boldness to my steps, to my hopes, to my fond dreams as I have never known before . . .

How strange it is to move into such a hackneyed idyll, to have arrived at a whole demi-world of emotions and appearances that conforms with such a well-known romantic convention and find it so vigorous and true! The swain in love, lying on the grass beneath the tree and singing love songs, is to me more a symbol of the utter rarity of pure delight than the false and fatuous convention it has become. It represents the coming of the exquisite and long-awaited moment, the moment of reward for a whole boyhood spent dreaming unhappily of love. It is the one consolation of being a youth in England, still! Though the cars and lorries were speeding by, I swung my arms in a romantic paradise that morning, and arrived at ten o'clock in the town of Rookhurst.

Without a pause I walked into a phone box and rang the number. Kate answered. 'Hello,' I said, and she replied, smiling, 'Hello, Charlie, where are you?' 'Rookhurst,' I said. 'No!' she said. 'I'm coming shopping in Rookhurst later with my mum. Will you still be there?' We arranged to meet in the car park. Where she is light and bright I am dark and heavy. Yet there was this convergence in our conversation, things were so easy for me, and though not filled with meaning or portent, they were serious and grave enough to her – I could tell – to make my heart sing with the belief in fortuity. For my awkwardness and her fluency had combined in one conversation as never before, the readiness to see each other, the unquestioning easiness with which it was all arranged filled my heart for the first time with a conviction of love's power. The power to change, to redeem, to recover, to mend . . . For me, so halting, so faltering, so unable to ask a girl I fancy for her address . . . this is salutary. For Paul, I must tell you, while happiness still has its mark on me, I begin to believe in an incredible and fortuitous fortune awaiting me. This happiness confirms a belief I have in providence. I would lie if I did not feel it, I would dishonour everything, I would spoil the happiness I have known if I did not confess that I believe happiness promises something more . . .

And then I went into a pub in the High Street and drank a pint of beer. I did not know how hot and thirsty I was; it was the most delicious thing I have ever tasted. As I drank it the sun was coming through the windows into the dusty, empty room. I looked out the window. This boring country town looked like something from the childhood of Abraham Lincoln! I walked to the car park. Though it was April, though it was only eleven thirty or so, the sun was hot. The town was very quiet, it being the middle of the week. The streets were empty except for one or two old ladies, crossing the road lower down the High Street. In a few minutes a little red car came into the car park, a brown hand waving out of the window at me. She ran over to me barefoot and kissed me and hugged me, it was the most enthusiastic, generous welcome I could conceive of. You cannot imagine how lovely it was to be greeted in this friendly way. Then I saw this squinting figure coming towards us, smiling lop-sidedly and looking me up and down, also friendly, also observant; this was Kate's mother. She admired my jacket, which was that old ceremonial guards jacket, like Sergeant Pepper's. The only thing I had with me. Kate was wearing faded bright orange dungarees and a torn white T-shirt. We were all laughing together almost immediately. We divided the shopping between us, Kate and I going in one direction, her mother in another. We met back in the car park twenty minutes later and drove to the farm.

For the remainder of the day I stayed by Kate's side, in such an elevation of spirits and tangible happiness as I cannot describe. And that day, as I remember it now, continued for ever. At moments I would wonder to myself: 'Did I only arrive here this morning?' and had to confirm the fact, though it was contrary to all my sensations of time. We did so much, visited so many places and people. First we did a bit of work in her mother's garden, hoeing between onions and parsley. We did a few chores and errands on the farm, like kids in a picture book. Fetching some logs in a wheelbarrow we met an old pair, who lived nearby, doing a bit of road-mending. They were huge and sunburned. Kate chatted to them for about ten minutes. Clearly they loved Kate, they talked so readily and openly with her. They laughed a great deal through their various complaints. We then thought we should go and visit my grandmother, because she wouldn't know where I had got to. So Kate and I walked down to the Rookhurst road and waited for a bus. On the way, two cars stopped and offered to give us a lift though they were obviously going in the wrong direction. One was a young man in a truck filled with chainsaws and fencing posts; he had a burry slow voice and ignored me completely. The other was a grey-haired woman, very neat and pleasant, to whom I was civilly introduced. We caught the bus to my grandmother's house, and spent the afternoon there. My grandmother, who is very objectionable as a rule, failed to notice how much she enjoyed talking with Kate and in fact failed to realise that she was making a new friend at all. (Later that week when I was back with her, she remembered this meeting, and after puzzling over it for a few moments, suddenly announced that she was pleased I had met her friend Kate at last, she couldn't remember when she had first met her, but they had been friends for ages . . . This was very funny and typical.) After drinking tea with my grandmother we carried an old wind-up gramophone and some old Dixieland records to a patch of sunlight in the garden. We stole a bottle of drink and drank and danced very fast. Oh, we were in love, or rather we were behaving like two people in love, but still I didn't quite dare touch her. Once we stood very close beside one another and could say nothing. At five o'clock we said goodbye to my grandmother and hurried back to the farm in a taxi. Her mother looked pleased I had returned as well. Kate had told me that her mother liked me, and that this made it much easier my being there. Her mother had made a meal of vegetables from the garden. The garden was beautiful; the house, an old dark squat stone farmhouse, looked out through small windows and small doors on to this garden and across a valley to a bank of wide downland.

After supper we left the house. As dusk fell we wandered among her mother's flowers; their scent and shade seemed to swell before me in the falling light. Then we walked through a gate, across a path, and into a wood through which we rambled for several hours. In the darkness I was slowly filled with that sense of incredulity and relief when fantasies are driven out by living fact, by breathing truth.

To be in a warm wood at night, with your heart beating thickly, is something that must be done, Paul.

To be in a little patch of wildness, stimulated to that fine alertness by the incredible density of life in a wood at night, and also cushioned with that sense of drugged disbelief your love feels on the first assurance of reciprocation coming like a warm stream into your veins. Ah! this idyll is too dark, too deep, too powerful for us to be familiar with it. The mild disorientation magnifies dark-enclosed sensibilities as the night awes love.

We were very close, our arms and shoulders brushing as we went along, occasionally one of us would trip or stumble and then the other would catch them, and then let go! It was relaxing to be spared the awkwardness of catching one another's eye. I felt she loved me already as much as I loved her, yet also felt the presence of other wild and dissonant claims on her affection. I am so naïve a lover, I didn't know how to behave in this darkness; to restrain myself, or express my love. It was Spenserian, the two of us walking through the dark wood; she so sure of the path, and I so lost. And in the dark there were many thought-filled silences between us which was as curious a joy as two people working very fast beside each other, untangling a knot in a rope in great haste and succeeding. I felt full of vision in those moments, and I debated if her selflessness might not inhibit the spontaneous impulse of her love. I anticipated the devotion between us would not soon be cemented; also that whatever reasons she had for keeping me from her would not be divulged. Though she could feel my love, it must go undeclared.

It sounds absurd to prepare yourself to meet a situation like this: to love so near to passion and yet not declare that love. Would we not even kiss? I wanted her so badly! It would be unsupportable and outrageous if I did not admire her as I do. Her character is so just, so fair — more so than anyone else — that I cannot suspect her of pettiness or of toying with me. If I knew her reasoning I would endorse it, however much it went against my favour. This is the selflessness of love. Something in her psyche requires she behave like this, and I have such respect for her that I will never ask her to explain what she doesn't choose to. And I can suffer the pain of restraint, perhaps more easily than others. I find a certain stoical pleasure in containing my love. It increases the joy, it drives the joy to my head, it forces me awake, it forces me alive.

The two instincts are so strong in her, the self-less and the self-denying, and the luxurious and the self-pleasing, that the question of my fate became intensely erotic in itself. As we walked side by side in the dark like brother and sister, the patina of my desire grew lustrous . . .

We returned to the house about midnight, our clothes torn and ripped by falls through brambles. Our skin scratched and torn. Laughing and very happy. Kate's mother was in bed, but not asleep for we could hear her coughing and rasping upstairs. We found a bottle of whisky and we lit a big fire. We sat in front of the fire and started to drink. I had the sensation of talking freely for the first time in my life; the ability to say what I felt and what I meant. Kate asked me what I was going to do with my life. I said I couldn't tell, and then I started talking about her. She resisted, and referred to herself in such abject terms that I was horrified. She called herself superficial, frivolous, dim, slow. I interrupted her again and again. You are not any of these things, I said, you are the reverse. You are extraordinarily intelligent though you don't express it to yourself – which is what everyone uses their intelligence for; you are extraordinarily perceptive though you don't make anyone aware of it – which is what everyone does with their perception. I went through everything. You are the richest person I have met, your virtues are the proper virtues, as they were meant to be, undemonstrative and affective. You are true beauty, I said, and for some reason it has been given to me to recognise this. You are the salvation of my world. I see the point of life in the way you live. It is harder than I believed, but it is better than I ever hoped to realise . . . I talked and talked in this vein and managed somehow to avoid declaring that I loved her.

Again she remonstrated with me, and abused

herself. And again I argued, and from chance I found her weak spot, for she started to listen to me now. I was telling her that she was *serious*. That this was a quality I valued above all others, and which was rarer in people than all others. That she was undoubtedly the most serious person I had ever met, and though she presented herself as a lightheaded hysteric, wild and extravagant, she was, more than anyone else, truly serious. Why? I couldn't tell why, but she had this unforced ability to think naturally and deeply on everything about her. She denied this, but I insisted, and even held up for comparison one or two observations she had made that day – of undeniable and extraordinary penetration – to the inane remarks on a similar theme remembered from days at school and university where seriousness is either a mask of insecurity or a badge of stupid ambition. But I knew more than just the paltriness of teenage affectations. For through my father, I said, I had met many of the world's most celebrated painters, poets and philosophers. I had talked with them and studied them, and they might all be impressive and interesting, but were not serious. They did not know the meaning of the word. They knew nothing about life as I had already learnt from her. When she expressed an opinion, one had the impression of a fine leaf of thought coming off an enormous lathe, which had been turning a great solid object with adamantine application and slowness . . .

And then, realising I had touched her very deeply, from where I was lying I stretched my arm towards her to embrace her. But my arm was left hanging in the air. So weird was this situation, I said, without knowing why: 'I am so happy I want to die.' Upon this instant, two things happened together. The first was – I felt – that her resistance suddenly collapsed, the second was a sharp noise from upstairs; instead of embracing me she fled the room. I then heard doors banging upstairs and her mother shouting. I heard Kate's voice answer soothingly, I heard her mother call her a 'fucking whore'. Lights went off upstairs. I waited for a few minutes, wondering if Kate would return, but after a quarter of an hour or so, with everything in the house quiet, I found a bed for myself and fell asleep.

I was allowed a hurried breakfast in the morning and then expected to leave. We had a solemn walk a hundred yards together, just enough for Kate to tell me that her mother was often impossible. I couldn't really question her; I would have liked to ask for what reason she let her mother's petulance eclipse the most sincere confessional of her life. Her mother was extremely powerful of course, and I wondered if a punitive selflessness had become the mainspring of many of Kate's actions. We promised to see each other soon in Edinburgh. We were both filled with despondency. A brief hug with an automatic squeeze of consolation and we parted.

I spent the morning walking slowly to the railway station and my dejection, which followed me as she walked by my side, vanished as soon as she left me. The rich, sure promise of happiness of the morning before returned undaunted. I stood a long time on the platform in a pool of sunlight, letting train after train pass me by and thinking of the previous day, its extraordinary pleasure and its astonishing chasms of sadness. How I have changed inside. How similar I remain.

28th April

Dear M,

I got back a few days ago. The air is fresh and very cold. It is like returning to the middle of winter, coming straight here from the balmy spring airs and breezes of Sussex. It is like travelling a season back in time. The spring I found so ravishing as it broke out around me in the hedgerows and along the verges of Sussex lanes will seep out around me here, but whether it will be more powerful for having been held longer in check, or whether it will feel like a weak reprise of a recent birth, I have no way of knowing. That depends on me! For the moment the snow is on the hills and the wind is even sharper than I remember it in December. Heavily cloaked and dressed up, I dragged my old motorbike out of the shed at the bottom of Tom and Mary's garden, and spent an afternoon in the damp, dark air getting it going. And then, at dusk, it fired up, just as the frost was settling on the roads, so I waited till the following morning, Sunday, and set out in the bright sunlight for a ride through the Pentland hills. The roads were slippy, and the ancient old bike coughed along slowly, never wanting to get going. I got extremely cold, but the country was beautiful. I cannot really bear to be in the town at the moment,

I want mud and green fields around me, but the severe weather makes it so difficult. If I was hardier, and tougher, I would be better able to stay outside a long time. As I spluttered shivering along the Pentland roads I came upon several little parties, striding breezily along. We waved; without stopping or talking I could tell they would make the round trip on foot from Edinburgh, some fifteen or twenty miles all told. It is common to meet people who will walk so far for a pleasure outing. My nervy old bike and me can bear about fifty minutes until we have to return home again, and then I remain frozen for the rest of the day. I will write again soon.

1st May

Dear Paul,

Following the day we spent together in Sussex I am with her more often. She has now introduced me to some of her friends, and most days I am able to spend a little time with her. Our friendship is now formalised, as it were, and this is a huge satisfaction to me. But I have misgivings too. Since her mother destroyed the most pregnant moment between us, I fear we might never reach such intimacy again. But for her mother's rage she would not have resisted me then, but now might resist me always. I do not know why.

Mary, who I lodge with, found me reading a book of poetry. 'Ah, you must be in love!' she piped mockingly! This is from Baudelaire:

Once, only once, loveable and sweet woman
Upon my arm your polished arm pressed
And on my spirit's dark background
That memory flashes now.

There are other misgivings. I know now she has a boyfriend. I am not surprised. She does not talk of him to me. Given her candour I take this as an honour – my love is even able to extract consolation from dismay! The only time I have seen her embarrassed is when someone asks about him in front of me. I do not know where he is, or how I have avoided meeting him.

A few days ago she discovered I had never been to her flat. She was uncomfortable then too, I suppose because she brings all her slightest acquaintances there. To correct this she therefore led me directly to the door of number 15 Barony Street. On the way she told me about Frank, who shares the flat with her, painting him in such enthusiastic and affectionate terms to allay my fears that he might be her lover. I knew he was not, I knew her boyfriend was called Tomas. A man opened the door to our knock, he was gentle and welcoming, despite an affected indifference to my arrival. This was Frank.

There was no Tomas, thank God! I think he must be away. But for his sake I do not think I will come here often. I was allowed a glimpse only, and had to drink the divine confusion of that wonderful place in one draught. The flat is – ah, I speak well about everything to do with her – the loveliest place I have ever been. These rooms are the incarnation of her effusive energy. Apparently untidy, and almost hysteric in its disarray, it is, in fact, the most deeply ordered home I have ever visited. No doubt I love her, and no doubt the visit was like being invited inside her body, but I could not have imagined anything to be so original, so exquisite, so comfortable, so delightful or so much the analogue to her character. It is a living dusty dream and nothing less than a demonstration of the great affective power of unbridled energy.

I have never called anything a work of art in my life. I have never seen such a thing. I have seen poems printed in books but their existence is intangible, they are not works, they are the memory of words. But this flat I would call a work of art. Oh, it gave me such insights; to look on the workings of someone who knows how to make beautiful things is the greatest privilege on this earth.

There was something Kate wanted to show me and as soon as we got in the flat she started to look for it, rifling through several shoe boxes stuffed with her collection of letters, cards, photographs. She became absorbed in her things and I moved around the flat. There was a fire and a mantelpiece, old carpet, old chairs, an old table and boxes. On the table what do you expect? Cups and plates! The regularity of the furniture made the powerful sensation of originality enigmatic. The chaos was warm; everything was marked with a feeling of her generous and abundant liveliness. One item especially caught my eye, a very obvious example of her taste perhaps, it was simply a towel rail with a loop towel on it. It was old, from the 1950s possibly, and the towel was a buttery yellow. This towel and rail, which would have appealed to any collector of kitsch, hung there straight, without irony or comment. I became strangely transfixed by this one thing and I spoke my thoughts out loud, and said in a way that would have struck anyone else as deeply stupid: 'What a beautiful towel that is; it hangs there just as it was meant to.' I felt like an idiot, who, lost in the confusion of his own impressions, wildly selects an inappropriate object to praise, because he cannot think what else to say. But Kate smiled as I said this, and patted my head as she walked by, giving me a feeling that if I have ever done or said anything which caused her to appreciate me, then this stupid remark about the towel was it.

Back at home I sat and thought about the flat, for its spirit had reminded me strongly of something but I could not remember what. I spent several hours rummaging through my thoughts, entirely happy, comparing the aesthetic of those rooms with everything I had ever admired. Eventually I discovered the comparison I had made. I was not surprised it took me so long, for on the surface no two things could be more unalike; but the comparison I had made was with those beautiful domestic interiors and still lives of Cézanne. You must know which I mean, the apples on a plate, on a table. I have always thought these pictures were painted in honour of a spirit of domestic organisation that was new, exquisite and entirely unselfconscious. A charm of domestic arrangement, that is highly aesthetic and simple, as elegant as a painting by Delacroix, and rustic as an autumn apple. When Cézanne first painted those apples with such care and with such sensuous plainness he was, I believe, admiring a tableau that someone else had set; it was more beautiful than anything he could have made himself. He was first of all evoking the genius of those hands that put the apples there, hands which were guided by a way of doing things for which he had abundant admiration. It is this honour of a whole way of doing things that is the huge and revolutionary charm of these paintings, that still has us swooning in galleries today. A style of arrangement that was pure and aesthetic, that blossomed throughout France and was more evocative, and more sumptuous, than any other of the grand stylistic innovations of the nineteenth century. The beauty of the fruit filling the whole poor room with beauty. The fruit becomes the poor man's painting; the poor man has a beauty finer than the rich man. Cézanne sees all this, his apology to all this beauty is to paint a picture! This style, which Cézanne was the first painter to admire, has in it a hint of a deep, inarticulate re-evaluation of beauty. A rejection of its formal value of display for the serene beauty of the interior life. I remember watching my grandmother arrange fruit with a wholly unconscious and cerebral care.

Barony Street has none of that wretched, tatty emulation of the flavours of provincial bohemian France. But, through the hysterical clutter, everything seems composed according to some deeply charmed aesthetic order.

8th May

Dear Paul,

Yesterday I bumped into Kate in the street – I always like it best when we see each other by chance – and we spent an evening in a bar called Bannerman's, which is where Terence likes to drink his Carlsberg Special Brew. To be together once with these two, the finest souls I have ever met, is to know I can never doubt again that I have lived. They are real, they are not dreams, they could not be dearer to me! Terence loves her, they laugh together so infectiously. He calls her 'my dear' and kisses her cheek with the most charming, blushing glee. The bar was full that night of English rowdies who also like the place. Kate knew them, and had a great deal of fun at their expense by teasing them. She cuts them very deep, and bewilders her victims by making them laugh at the same time. They are robust and enjoy the power of her wit. Every now and then they would confirm their solidarity to one another by launching into a crude, loud old song. Terence listened and laughed, was enjoying himself, joined in the choruses and then, during a lull, suddenly slapped his thigh and sang: 'Rejoice and be glad, for the springtime has come, we can throw down our shovels and go on a bum, Hallelujah I'm a bum, Hallelujah bum again, Hallelujah give us a handout to revive us again.'

After this evening in the pub, Terence pushed off and we went back to Kate's flat. Frank was there again to open the door for us. Kate seems to have no key of her own, or else she loses it for I have never seen her unlock her own door. Frank, lovely Frank, is devoted to her. He poured us both a beer, he asked us about our evening. He knew all the people we had met, but I am not sure if this isn't largely through her descriptions. It seems that the part of his life which he enjoys most is that part which he lives vicariously through her. He laughed at her stories which were brilliant; she catches everyone so well. Her descriptions are so accurate and so funny. I wonder at the cleverness she has not only to observe so much, but to retell it so wittily. It is simply I suppose that I have never met a sophisticated person before. She is, in a proper sense, a very sophisticated person. I am in continual astonishment at my own dullness. I was there with her. I saw the same things, I heard the same things, but I could not have described it as she did in a million years. And this is a continual stream of invention. As I am wondering at the cleverness and precision of one description, she is started on another, and my intention to commit the first to memory is lost while my wonder grows for the next.

And if I could remember a fraction of her

descriptions then how my letters to you would be improved. You would laugh, you would see the world I saw, you would observe the thoughts passing across the faces that I saw but which I cannot describe now.

I fear she must find me boring, my sense of inadequacy with her is so pronounced that I begin to stutter when I talk. I am kept abreast of the present, as it were, only by the vivacity of my excitement. When we were alone that evening she looked at me in silence for a while, trying to find the right words for something she wanted to say. She patted my head and said, 'You know, Charlie, I think you are a wonderful man, I really do.' She didn't know how to say any more.

We drank beer. We danced. A knock on the door and Derek Kidd came in and suddenly our consumption of alcohol increased madly. We all danced. Derek Kidd is an old alcoholic Dundee bohemian, who is so sweet to be with and so boring to talk to, that when he turns up there is nothing to do but dance. He can dance like no one else. He stands on the floor with his bottom pushed out and his elbows crooked, his bald head down, like a cockerel giving birth, moving with sublime slow jerks in an old London blues style from the 1960s. After a while Kate pushed him out of the door. We sat down and we talked till it was late, then we got up and danced again, just the two of us. Time strung out, the alertness we have in each other's company makes it possible for us to continue in this pattern, talking and dancing, for ever. We are like two lovers frozen at a certain point in their courtship. It was very late. I should have gone long before, I should have left her, but really, being alone with her, nothing could have brought me to leave willingly.

My refusal to leave was a species of inconvenience to her. I knew there was no question of sleeping with her; I knew she wouldn't sleep with me. But I also felt that she liked my being there, and that she knew I would never be a nuisance to her, or pester her. I am sure she has this confidence in me, I do not know why. I can only imagine that no one else understands her so well as I, no one else appreciates her continual gifting of energy and understanding to others. In a way, by demonstrating that I am happy not to sleep with her, I validate my admiration. It is more serious to her.

Anyhow, I continued staying, as it were. She must have been very tired for I knew she had been out all the night before, but she did not flag. At four in the morning someone knocked on the door and two men, strangers to me and friends to Kate, came in. For some reason I was not afraid that her boyfriend would suddenly appear. She never speaks about him to me. Though he is not in Edinburgh, I realise he might return at any moment.

Anyhow, at four in the morning, these two men

dropped in. They had some drink and we all sat and talked. They had been out, they were drunk, and they had seen her light on, and although they didn't have much appetite for it, they had clearly had the idea to come and keep their night going a bit longer by chatting with Kate. I liked these two men so much and so quickly that I felt sure neither of them came with any hope of having sex with her. And though, in the circumstances, it does not sound very likely, I think I am right. One was a teacher at the university, Ogden, young, friendly and very drunk. Dave was a huge, handsome black man with an ironic wink that was penetrating and slow. Our intimacy interrupted, I suddenly felt my exhaustion. Kate, however, stayed awake as if it were ten in the morning, though almost nothing of interest was going on, or being said. It is typical of her that she next suggested about four-thirty in the morning that we go for a walk. Everyone liked this idea. Ogden had been talking about Warriston cemetery, which I had never heard of. Kate suggested we go and visit it, so we did. It was only about ten minutes' walk away, but in a direction in which I had never gone. The friends talked together and I walked beside Kate. We got to the cemetery, and walked among the graves in the dark night, distracted and absorbed, and without a thought for the dead. A sudden noise, a cracking of a twig, not ten feet away, startled us. We all heard it, and we all started, and Kate and I suddenly caught each other by the hand. The fright passed in an instant, and there remained only the proof of some automatic correspondence between us, that in the dark, without having thought of it, our hands found each other with absolute certainty. I had opened my fingers and closed them on hers, just as she had done with mine. It was exhilarating, and delicious like nothing has ever been delicious before. It was an unequivocal demonstration of closeness between us, but it was also full of foreboding. It was so intense a display of affection but also so circumspect. We said goodbye to Dave and Ogden and walked back towards Barony Street, but still not talking about ourselves even while we were holding hands. At her door I said goodnight, and pushed off to my lodgings, realising as I did so that the expedition to the cemetery was in part a way of getting me out of the flat. It was an emphatic demonstration that she would not sleep with me or let me into her bedroom. I said goodbye, we embraced, it was a sad, warm moment. I knew her boyfriend was very present in her mind. I do not know what she thinks of him. I cannot believe she loves him, but then perhaps she is capable of loving many people.

15th May

Dear Paul,

We talk endlessly. It is all we allow ourselves to do. Often we lie very close to one another on the floor, and Kate will stroke my hair while I talk to her. I have never spoken sincerely to anyone before, I think. Then, when it is very late and we must sleep, we want to stay together. I climb into her bed, clothed, and we lie in a sort of ring, with only our heads and feet touching. The press of my forehead against hers and our feet touching brings a calm of unity to me. She falls asleep almost instantly, and I lie in a heaven of reflection and gladness beside her.

Last night I told her a story of how, once – only once! – when I was eight years old, I fell very power-fully in love. This was with an extraordinary girl, also called Katie. At that age she seemed to be much older than me, but was at the most a year or two only, I suppose; wild and tall, with intense calm blue eyes and a high, airy voice, full of intonation. She lived with eight or nine brothers and sisters in a large broken-down house in Scotland. She kept a kestrel as a pet, who sat on a perch in the middle of the lawn while we played. Once, I think it was the first day I had been to the house, while everyone was playing around me in the sun, and I remember Katie had made us take off all our clothes, I sat watching the kestrel, about ten feet away, I suppose. I loved the bird; it was through the bird we had made friends so quickly. It was tied by a leather lead to its perch, but it had pecked it through, for suddenly it threw itself off the perch and dived for my head. The shackle snapped, and it swooped down towards me and then soared out above me. I could have put out my hands and caught it. It sat for several days in a tree, ignoring our calls for it to return, the circle of children heaping little dainties for it in a pile on the grass.

This girl had a tender wildness that was quite fascinating. Everyone loved her for her spirit and her independence; and for some reason she loved me. She did not make a fuss of me, as it were, but she used to like to be with me, and did not try to get away from me like the others did. Inside, I was passionate about her. I mainly remember how beautiful I thought she was; I only have to think of her name and the delicious feeling she made inside me returns. Her presence was exotic and quiet, she knew that she went very deep into me, had come right in, as it were, and was pleased and interested with the rearrangement she made of my insides.

It was hot, that summer, and Katie insisted everyone keep their clothes off almost all the time. I remember there was a subtle wickedness to this nudity, a rebellion against the foulness of adult minds.

Hers was a strange knowing innocence, a wild subversion of experience.

I have seen her once since that summer, and do not often think of her. If I do, however, I am astonished at how deeply I still love her, and how extraordinary she must be still. It was the coincidence of her name being Kate that brought her back to me. I could tell Katie how much I loved this girl, and how grateful I was to have passion re-excited. It was my way of telling Kate that I loved her for a number of reasons, which all coincided, which awoke pieces of my past, which resolved a whole number of thoughts of my present.

All this Kate absorbed very solemnly, without saying anything. I was trying to describe her looks to Katie, and I said that, if anything, she was like a Burne Jones figure, but in her eyes shone a breezy innocence so mild it seemed sometimes inexpressibly defiant. And then I stopped, realising I was touching on something that upset Kate, as she listened. She thought for a long while, and looking down – I remember her chin bobbing, like a little bird on the brink of tears – said to me that she had never been innocent. I had never heard Kate's voice so toneless and flat.

I was shocked, for the awfulness of this truth not only affected me in myself, but made the stark comparison between us even greater, and I said in answer, 'And I have never been anything but innocent!' It was a moment coloured with a profound desperation, for it was the truth about ourselves, and a mark of the difference between us, and the huge gulf which separates us and which will never be closed. I understand more now about the bond between us. She has never been innocent, and it is the opportunity to redeem the misgivings of this fact that I present her with. This is the glistening coronal of our friendship, this is what binds us; the chasteness of our secret love.

20th May

Dear Paul,

I have much time to consider these events, and understand the why of them. It is her decision we should get no closer. I have no doubt she is right, I have never seen her be wrong about anything, or make a mistake in any of her judgements. The greater the difficulty she has to find a reason for something, the more certain it becomes in my eyes. Even when her actions defy logic or explanation – of which the trip to her mother is the only one of a thousand instances of this that you know about – there is no question that she was right to do them. The reasoning is buried too deep in her conscience to emerge, and I revere nothing so much as her conscience. This faith in her is an absolute condition of my love. My life is committed henceforth to proving that I am right to trust her now. I believe in time I will understand all this, and be vindicated, though it take until my death.

Provisionally, I understand love as an argument between two souls, both of whom need the lesson the other teaches. She needs the touch of my innocence, and I need the touch of her experience. These qualities cannot combine without being ruined, therefore we must stay separate to preserve our meaning to each other. It is a strange sort of love, but real.

Her life is stronger than my own. I am aware of being overpowered by her. But I need this. She is the revelation of life which I did not have the power to generate myself. She is the embodiment of the life which I would have made for myself had I been strong enough.

This opinion is generated by my understanding of myself. Ever since boyhood my life has been a series of encounters with evidence of my own weakness and error. Nevertheless I have preferred my own precepts in the task of strengthening myself because no others seemed as good. I have admired many people, in many ways and for many reasons, but until now never met someone who overrules entirely my faith in my own instincts, who proposes a better way to confront all these difficulties. I have done nothing stupid, and made no huge mistakes, but I have been too bound up in contrivance, of which she is the antithesis. Her example is just what I need to grow, to complete my education and development.

Psychologically, love arrives just at that period when we are coming to the close of our character's development. In a terrible crisis, love finally settles the question of how to conclude the long-conducted experiment of our conscience.

24th May

Dear Paul,

My situation with her girlfriends is peculiar. They realise we are devoted, but do not quite know, or dare ask, how far our friendship goes. (I do not believe she talks about me with anyone!) Also, she is continually pestered by lecherous men, never a day but she receives ten invitations to go out alone with one of them. These men are all terribly keen to sneak in and wean her from her boyfriend while he is not here. I find myself quite indignant on his behalf. They see me and wonder about me, I watch them weighing up the evidence and deliberating whether I am a secret lover and a rival to their plans, or a sort of eunuch slave. This is what they put Frank down for, and it is a vile misrepresentation. He has become, after you, my greatest friend. I love him and he loves me.

The confusion of her friends about me is wonderful. What is obscure to them is as clear as daylight to the rest of the world. Today – yesterday, or was it the day before? – we spent all night dancing in a dance hall, at a concert, in a huge crowd. I received a thousand smiles and winks from strangers all around me. We were wild together in public. Young men slapped my back. 'You're in with a chance there, pal,' one man said — as a joke of course — and all the women smiled to themselves to see us dance.

28th May

Dear Paul,

We love, and yet we pretend we do not. Why? I know why, but still the extraordinariness of the situation threatens to overwhelm me. I am only happy when we are together, but sometimes I find it hard to speak with her. In this anguish of constraint I feel close to breakdown, and yet that would betray her. She gives me strength to bear this restraint but only when I am with her, then it is the easiest thing in the world to think of keeping apart from her. But when I am alone, then I am truly desolate, then I feel the need of her touch and her warmth.

I cannot collapse, I would never forgive myself if I did. I would ruin myself, for it would mean her example to me would have been powerless. I think of her strength in coping with her father's death, and her consolation of her mother, which requires forbearance a thousand times greater than the forbearance required of me now, and I know I must not collapse. It would indict all she teaches me, and then I would be ruined, absolutely ruined.

30th May

Dear Paul,

I am restored from my gloom. We have been talking so much together these last few days, there is always noise and activity when I am with her. Though the corridor is dark and the windows dirty, her flat is like a large square house beside the sea where all the rooms are filled with the fresh noise of wind, birds and waves. When she goes out of the room, I remain lying where I am, and, falling into a silent reverie, let my thoughts stroll. A change has come over my companionship with my self, I no longer think falteringly; it is as if my thoughts put on boots and stride for the hills. A briskness, quiet and supple, and a determination, natural and easy, animates my reverie. Then, at these moments, completely at ease, as relaxed and as preoccupied as if I were asleep and dreaming, I stalk above our grassy world like a wind in shirtsleeves or a cloud in trousers. A freedom of imagination has come into my blood. Love is eternal, beauty is eternal, truth is eternal. With this conviction in my heart I will henceforth meet the world. I am equipped with a stoic resolve to battle my way through life! Alone if I have to! Onward!

1st June

Dear Paul,

I have to think about Kate's boyfriend. Wherever I go people ask me if I know him. The negligence in their voices warns me of the terrible jealousy he will feel when he learns of me. He will suspect me at the first mention of my name. As yet he must know nothing about me – or he would be here! He is in London, working to become an artist, a singer or a writer. This confusion of ambitions is perhaps vain, but not so deluded as it sounds for there is no doubt he is a man of extraordinary gifts. He has led an interesting life; orphaned when very young, and barely educated, he persuaded his brother-in-law, an estate agent, to rent him a flat very cheaply when he was sixteen years old. So he moved into 15 Barony Street twelve years ago, and he has lived here ever since, writing, painting, getting stoned. The flat is littered, or decorated rather, with his things. Once they were sharp and precise, now they are all scuffed and old, but there remains a peculiar hauntingness to the neatness and modesty of these little productions. They are overlooked by all the visitors to the flat for they are lost in Kate's exuberant clutter, but I am deeply impressed with every one of them. Partly out of respect for Kate's taste in people, and partly from fear, I have formed an admiration for him. His poems, many of which are pinned to the wall, are very striking and sharp, mild and astringent, gentle and needling at the same time. I know of no one else who has so succinct and epigrammatic a hand. There is no doubt he is gifted. There is one small painting done directly on to the wallpaper. It has been there a long time, and is now very dirty. No one looks at it. In subject it is very obvious, a stylised reworking of a Piero della Francesca thing, done in block colours. I didn't notice it for a long time but when I did see it I was captivated. It has that extraordinary inconspicuousness of really beautiful things. He has this. I feel attracted to him. I want to know him. It must be frustrating for him, struggling to make it down south, where no one cares for talent.

Sometimes I am at Katie's flat when parcels arrive from him of letters, presents, things he has made or bought. These also always have something to wear, and Katie will pull it out and put it on first, before she opens anything else, or reads any of the letters or messages. He chooses perfect things for her. A woolly hat, or a cardigan this week, pale blue and lustrous, that she makes look ravishing. He understands her as well as I. I cannot tell you how beautiful she is.

He is also vain, ergo he is jealous. There is a series of little photographs of him taken in a photo booth which he has decorated with pencil and blue biro. Little stripes and checks to his shirt. A spider's web of lines that magnifies his charming face, distant and distracted in the portrait. 'The young man is far away . . .' is written around the edge, 'his thoughts precede him home . . .' The strange doctored glee of these photographs emphasises that he is very handsome. I have the feeling that everything he touches is touched simply and artfully. His tiny hand-writing is strangely unsettling, and I get the shivers wondering how a man with such an acute obses-sion with himself and with his property will deal with me.

Yesterday I picked up a picture and turning it round read a description in his hand of Kate and him making love. It was a great shock, I had made every effort to drive the thought of the two of them sleeping together from my mind. I put the picture back as if I had been scalded, but today I went over to it and read the whole poem. A piece of madness which I do not know whether to interpret as pruri-ence or intense self-mortification.

5th June

Dear Paul,

Paradise is a world into which one gets dragged by hooks. I have been made intensely happy and miserable at the same time.

Over a few weeks I have realised Kate was becoming agitated. Something was weighing on her mind that she could not bear to tell me. Like a child who cannot suspect the obvious, I did not realise what was about to happen. I watched her growing nervousness with anxiety for her, and no apprehension for myself.

Eventually I put my hand on hers and asked her what was wrong. You can tell me anything, I said, you need to tell me something, tell me what it is. We were in her room. She looked down and said, 'Tomas is coming back. He is coming back to live here.'

I asked her how she felt about this.

'I'm very unhappy,' she said, 'for myself and for you.'

'Could we not do something about it?' I asked. She said nothing, and so I added, 'Would you like to come and live with me?' 'No,' was all she said.

I was shocked and I was not shocked. I had been living in such a precarious dream that I was not surprised it was all over.

I thought a long time in silence about what she said, and then slowly we began to talk about it. I was relieved, I think, that we were talking properly about our friendship for the first time. Seriously, with the actual facts of our lives open for discussion. She said, 'I won't be able to see you . . . so much, or for a while at least.' And then she added, 'I will miss you very much.' This was meant to console me, and it did the reverse. Is that all, would she only miss me? I was never so hurt. I answered her bravely, and crossly. 'I will be all right,' I said. 'It will be fine. I just won't come round here every day.' And then I lay down on the bed, and hid my anger that she would only miss me. But I love her so much, soon I was telling her that I could, if it were necessary, never see her again. I love you, I said, and I have hoped you love me. The love I feel for you is so powerful, there is nothing I could not do. I have grown used to loving you and not having you. My love is measured in how little of you I have. The less I have of you the more I love you. If I loved you less, I could not renounce you. You have given me such strength, as you will now discover. While making this chivalric geste to chastity I was coating myself with a strange and erotic perfume.

And then I said I had to go. She was crying, and she took my hand. She pulled me towards her and kissed me. This was my first kiss. I cannot describe the shock of delight, or the overwhelming deliciousness of kissing someone you love with all your heart for the first time. For several hours, another three hours at least, we kissed on that bed; the arrival of physical passion was our farewell. For the first time I didn't want to make love with her, I only wanted to kiss her. And then I had to get up and go.

6th June

Dear M,

I have recently been doing what I should be doing, which is reading history seriously. I have a great appetite for work all of a sudden. However, my desire to go into the past as an explorer, pushing a canoe up a creek, is impossible. There is only one way into this country and it is on board a huge and over-serviced liner.

And you must join a large tour party. And here we all are as the boat steams into harbour, we lean on the rail of the giant ship, we lean over the rail, we peer as deeply as we can into the shadows behind the foreshore – in competition with our neighbours who are behaving in exactly the same way – in desperation to have the satisfaction of having a private thought! I must escape the big ship. 'Get me away from this present,' I beg. 'Show me the balconies, the trees and the terraces of another time . . .'

8th June

Dear M,

Yesterday I found a book in the library which carried me away. It is called *Life and Culture in Medieval Europe*, by Charles H. Haskyns. It was published in 1920, in America, and the last time someone looked into it was in 1956. It contains a marvellous treasure, which has been exciting me very much. It is a collection of student letters from Paris in the twelfth century, when the schools of theology were exploding into the first university. When tens of thousands of young men, from all over Europe, began arriving on top of one another to study. Study became furious, ambitious, vainglorious; boys hurled into this swarming world sensed the uncertainty of everything! Nothing has changed; it is extraordinary how the life of the student of those days is so much like the student life of today, except that today, counting ourselves free and independent, we choose to be oblivious of ourselves and our surroundings.

These medieval clerks resembled us so much. Early in their existence they were looked on as a species of human ant. Collectively notorious for their arrogance, self-absorption and riots. Individually each child is wholly lost in this group characteristic; they stress in their letters home how formless, how characterless they remain, they hint they are beginning seriously to think about the future – always a sign of tender panic!

They are so early, these letters, written before Dante, before anyone had really begun to attempt emotive descriptions of things or people. This makes them more emotive than anything else, but still utterly straightforward. Often they are little more than a list of items the student needs; dried white peas, chalk, cloth for gowns, a kettle, lambskins. As you read over these letters you see these things very vividly; the leather as tough as steel, the iron as malleable as pastry, everything is organic, everything is stiff with dust and age, everything will endure a long time. You feel the frail, young students in the Paris rooms, summoning to their imaginations the sturdy totems of their homes, wrapping around their childish souls the stiff coats of their grandfathers. It is a moment of incredible poignancy.

I took the book to one of my teachers because I thought he would be interested in the letters. Quite soon I found I was in an argument with him and I started recommending them with exaggerated emphasis: 'They give me understanding,' I said. 'More than all the books on Thomas Aquinas . . . These letters have strange gifts of revelation . . . I am glad I read them, they have given me some permanent gain, some insight into the world which means something to my own condition . . .'

And I was doubted. So I babbled on some more about what it was these student letters had given to me that nothing else had. I can't remember everything I said, but it came out in a great flow. How given the effectiveness of education which started with this university, it is remarkable how little attention is paid to the world or the milieu of the students. This organic world is an atmosphere of sensations, it has altered very little in seven hundred years; it is of especial and crucial importance in the development of so many great and powerful minds. There are literally no books on the subject. There is only a great embarrassment from this early beginning in Paris until the present day. And I do not understand why. There are no modern appraisals or studies of this world; there never was any discussion of it. I tried to make him realise how remarkable it was that there was barely any mention of this world until Shakespeare writes *Hamlet*. And, of course, it was to make Hamlet feel himself so negligible, despite being a prince, that Shakespeare made Hamlet a student. He disputed that, and asked me what I was trying to say. I said I was interested in this formal period in which the individual, the sensitive, emotive individual, acquires some trace of the obliviousness with which the world regards him. 'This is a moment, a transition, I sense has occurred during the student days of many fascinating and fulsome lives. I feel it in Montaigne, I feel it in Jean-Luc Godard.' He laughed; I don't care.

Sometimes I think I might want to get away from here. My teachers tell me my enthusiasms spoil my objective grasp. They are ridiculous, and are serious about nothing. Typical scene, three professors on a train, every one of them reading the latest John le Carré!

12th June

Dear Paul,

Oh, he has returned. I can say no more. I must keep this love to myself though it wants to explode out of me. I explore the city. I have such thoughts . . . Discovering I can bear the unhappiness has led me to make the discovery that love, in truth, is most powerful when it frustrates us. It is most productive of inspiration. Deprived of her company, I am shown what exists of her in everyone else. It is like that Shakespeare sonnet in reverse:

> *Thy bosom is endeared with all hearts,*
> *Which I by lacking have supposed dead;*

Rather than finding all the dead virtues of the world reborn in the one I love, I find her virtues alive in the people who swarm about me. This is a contingency I suppose Shakespeare was never so love-deprived as to discover! I am denied her, but in her place I am brought to a most extraordinary sensation of intimacy with people everywhere. As if I was connected by love to everyone, absurd as this sounds. I walk through Edinburgh distinguishing in everyone qualities that amaze and astonish me. This cloud of joy continues to inflate inside me. I cannot describe the particularity of each sensation . . .

I am in heaven . . .

14th June

Dear Paul,

Did I not end my last letter by saying I am in heaven? Well I was wrong. I have found the missing heaven on earth. Only now do I understand that I will keep this love forever. Because of this terrible grief and pain I feel, the intoxicating excitement of my emotions and thoughts is seared into me, and will remain as a record of what love means forever. I have not the misfortune to feed and forget, which is the custom, which is how these beautiful souls which surround me came to be so oblivious of their beauty, and all the other fine truths they conceal about themselves. They have loved and they have enjoyed their love and its meaning has spilled out of them.

I have said before, I know, that love is a dispute between two souls, an argument that no other force in the world could bring you to conduct . . . More of this later, I am too inspired to philosophise! I feel every day more steeply elevated, more ominously charged . . . like a comic book hero, who receives some terrible power on account of an accident which befell him at a formative age! I beg you to believe I suffer the most incredible pain I have ever known.

Her company is a physical addiction, and I am now suffering terrible pains of deprivation. I cannot sleep, I can barely eat, I cannot talk with anyone without breaking out into fits of bodily shaking. I cry for hours and hours each night in my room. I hide myself from everyone who knows me, and cause the most tremendous anxiety among all those who have some care of me. Mary will not be allayed. No one will listen to my pleadings, that though I am physically racked and distraught, mentally I live on a plane of continual excitement that has rendered me supersensitive to the beauties with which the world so richly abounds.

O I am grateful to her.

14th June

Dear M,

Something has happened to me. I cannot tell you quite how important it is to me. But I love and I do not love. I am in heaven and I am in hell.

LOVE is finding in one thing the fullness of everything we have left out of ourselves. In the suddenness of the discovery we realise what it is to be whole, and so an idea of universal completeness is born for the first time in our hearts, which we identify with this one singular figure. This is how one small thing becomes the representation of everything. In the thing we love, we love the universal life. We love this person because they give the fullest account of the universe, of which we have previously only the vaguest notion. The truth of the world, its extraordinary beauty and symmetry, reveals itself to us seldom: when we are children mostly in momentary bubbles of perception, when we are grown in passionate feints upon our feeling. Our insights are occasional, rare, disruptive, and we are disturbed by the impersistence of beauty. But love is like a film, everything that is true is brought together in a sequence, a coherent sequence that one can follow; one laughs, one cries as one follows the story, you forget about yourself! You forget you are doing nothing. Everything you know but have never had the words to express is suddenly speaking to you. Language becomes a new language!

P.S. Reading through what I have written I think it might sound a complete jumble to you. In fact it is precise and exact, what I say. I also think it is true, or rather, it is true for me . . .

17th June

Dear Paul,

Only from earth can we discover the way to heaven and the passage to hell. My hours switch between brightness and shadow, excitement and gloom. I spend the days pushing my self through the streets where nothing happens, gathering jewels more intense, more pointed than the diamonds of Croesus. My blood is enriched, I spend my joy freely as I go, and return at dusk, poor and exhausted, to my room. There I draw the curtain and light a candle, and sit in the stillness of my thoughts a very long time. At the present Time sits on me like a veil. Through the long suspension of life of these rich hours I recall every instant we spent together, and in the recreation of these memories I recover a greater delight than I experienced at the time.

I read, and I drink in the memory of other loves!

> *Que j'aime voir, chère indolente,*
> *De ton corps si beau . . .*

I am beginning to be grateful in a number of different ways that it was an entirely sexless relationship. The first reason is that this draws me on, this keeps me alive. Were it not for the possibility of a delight greater than any I have ever known, I could not persuade myself there were any reason to stay alive.

But also, I am grateful that the sexlessness has given me such intense life in others. My love is not my own, it shares its pain and beauty with the living and the dead. Through my grief I live so richly, so abundantly.

The sexlessness of our love was the strangest part of it all, and by making our love more personal to us and unique, makes me love it and care for it all the more. I love my love, I caress it, and feed it, and worry so deeply for it.

I thank God I have been writing to you, for otherwise I could not confess this loss to anyone. Seemingly I have lost nothing, because she withheld herself. Had I not written of the swelling of my infatuation, how could I ask you to believe that such strong emotions attached to so unphysical a relationship?

I can't remember everything I have written to you, but I feel that I must have expressed somehow, somewhere, the fruit of the magnification of desire. Sexual prohibition caused such sublimation of my desires that the memories have now more body than the occasions they recall. The rareness of our touch, the very few occasions when our hands met, or our bare arms brushed each other, are branded so deeply in my memory that I cannot recall them without recovering the complete physical sensation.

> *Once, only once, loveable and sweet woman*
> *Upon my arm your polished arm pressed*
> *And on my spirit's dark background*
> *That memory flashes now!*

One time we lay down together on the floor late at night, and were talking, and her belly was bare. I loved her so much, but of course I had never seen her naked. I had barely seen any part of her naked, not even her belly, but then somehow, suddenly, it was bare, and more beautiful, and more sensuous than I could imagine anything else could be. I put my head close and began to smell its scent. I did, and though this was sheer desire, it was desire for her belly. This was no preliminary petting; with her belly beneath my nose I had everything in the world I wanted. I had never seen anything that looked so inviting to touch, or so beautiful. The heat of her belly, when I first touched it with my lips, startled me so that I gasped. The warmth of her body generated a warmth in me; our skin, when it touched, burned.

Nothing else existed for me, but this beautiful planet of her belly on which I had landed. All that happened was that I rested my face against her belly for a while one night. I could not have asked for more delight.

I identify now with those pitiful men you read of who used to get so excited over the glimpse of an ankle. We all understand how sexual suppression displaces desire from object to object, but now, in this porn-infested world, this sublimation of desire, this pursuit of fugitive eros, feels strangely clean.

I have developed a taste for the body that is sensual and ideal. I look at photographs of Greek *kouroi*, which I discover are superior many thousands of times to any other sculpture. Though all are youths and none of them complete, they suggest her.

I have no doubt that the sexual proscription enhanced my sensitivity to the eternal life of beauty. I feel the presence of antique love, more strongly than I feel the presence of love in the living world. I am surrounded by living beauty, but I feel no love around me.

There is a moment in a version of *Aladdin* that I read which has Aladdin fall in love at first sight with a girl who is as beautiful as a slender moon. It says that until that moment he had always thought all women were just like his mother. I do not believe such charming or innocent people still exist. I look at the pale moon and I see Kate.

I have, of course, only one dream, that something should happen to bring her back to me. That we could fall into each other's arms.

Dear Paul,

At the end of last week I was in my room when a knock came on my door. In the street was a car full of Kate's friends. Would I come with them to a party? Kate had asked them to bring me. They told me Tomas would be there. I went. He knew more about me than I expected. He is mysterious, or rather he means to impress me with his penetration. He introduced me to every passing friend, as a way of conveying his changing estimation of me; to someone he would say as they walked by, 'Hey, meet Charlie. Charlie is an oracle who can see into the past but not into the future,' or some such absurdity, and to another he would say, 'Here is a man I expect will need watching very closely.' His conversation is made up of threats dressed up as compliments, while he smiles blandly. I do not see how she could like such a man. I asked him about his time in London. Needless to say things hadn't worked out. I told him I was sorry, but not surprised. 'Why?' he asked. I told him I had admired those poems and paintings of his that I had seen in his flat, and knew they were too artful and too original to score in London. The world is only a bitch if you want to get on, I said. And then it is the worst bitch imaginable. People of talent are despised,

I said, because the world is so sick. Especially London. Kate was there, but I didn't speak to her. I left soon after. Tomas asked me to Barony Street, he said we've got some things to go over. It was uncomfortable, but less so than it might have been.

I did go next day, and have been going back. So, strange to say, I've been seeing my friends Tomas and Kate a good deal. At first it was harder for me to sit in a room with the two of them than it would be for me to sit in a room underwater. It began as a charade. Tomas, as he said, had a lot of things to 'go over'. As far as I can work it out, he returned and discovered that the girl he loves (and he loves her passionately) had made a new friend. Everywhere he goes he hears this new person's name. He soon learns this boy was not just everyone's new friend, but was particularly his girlfriend's friend. He works out they must have been together a huge number of times for so many different people to have met him. He realises that a few times they were alone together. He interrogates Frank, perhaps bullies him, and Frank admits that he did, sometimes, stay in Kate's bedroom. Kate eventually satisfies him that she did not sleep with this boy, that he is dear to her, but not a lover. Then he wants to meet me.

At first he greeted me like a Victorian father, who, planning to ruin his daughter's love for an unsuitable man, means to expose them both to the endless tedium of his sitting room. But such deliberate scheming was short-lived. Soon he had to talk about himself. I listen to his vast ambitions and his desperate hopes. It allows me to be near Kate.

Only by appearing at my most unassuming do I have any chance of seeing my love.

Dear Paul,

You are sweet to me to show such patience and kindness. To read my letters so thoroughly, and to think so hard about them. I understand your question. I do not know why she has behaved like this, it is a mystery. You were absolutely within your rights to ask why she let me fall so deeply in love with her. I confess I have no answer.

You are right too when you remark that for me the deprivation has become a kind of quest, which I win by staying alive, and right to ask me what could be the point of deprivation for her. I don't know. I don't know what she is thinking, if she is happy or miserable. I know she can conceal her feelings completely. You pay me the greatest honour ever paid to me – not to doubt she loves me. I marvel at your goodness, I cannot believe how lucky I am to have such a friend as yourself. I love you absolutely, Paul.

It is perhaps an elaborate fantasy, but I think that her loyalty to her boyfriend is connected with her self-recrimination over her father's death and that it stems from her mortification that her father died assuming she preferred to be with friends than with him. This has led her to restrain self-interest. She will never fail to be dutiful now. Wherever there is a conflict between obligation and her pleasure, pleasure will lose.

I have a feeling that the only way she could persuade her boyfriend to try and realise all his vast hopes was to promise that she would remain true to him while he was away, and that for nothing in all the world will she break this promise. There is a purposefulness in her decisions that is incredible, and disregards all thought of pain or self. I admire her for her denial of me. I do not know how through these cool privations she still appears so warm, and still is able to dress herself with the most luxurious and licentious taste of anyone in the world.

I am kept alive by the thought she secretly loves me more than this man. But even so, I don't know what on earth this means. I could not love as much as this, and let my lover endure the pain I feel.

Paul,

We see things only once, we feel things only once. The dullness of our perception is because everything is so familiar to us. When we see something original, we see it all in a glance, and then we never see it so completely again.

We are seldom interested in ourselves. When we love, when we are moved by love, then we forget ourselves and find ourselves interesting at the same time. Yes, we find ourselves interesting, at last!

I look around me and see people doomed to boredom by self-love; complaining the world is familiar and uninteresting. It is because of our devotion to ourselves, our attachment to ourselves, that we are so bored and listless.

We are too dull to wake up, we need the truth of love to live, and it comes only once. And it comes very quickly, and it comes clothed in pain and we fling our arms at it as a stage puppet flings its arms at a ghost. I do not know how, but I know it is true, that I have caught hold of love and will cling on to it forever.

27th June

Dear Paul,

Do you know of the library angel? That being which hands you books wherein lies the very thing you wanted to be searching for? And opens the page for you, and guides your eye to the very line?

Well today, while trying to find something to interest me, the title of a book caught my eye: *John Keats's Dream of Truth*. I know a little Keats, I know nothing about his dream of truth. The book fell open in my hand and I began to read a paragraph's commentary on 'The Pot of Basil', which poem opens almost immediately describing the feeling of love between noble Isabel and the servant Lorenzo:

> *They could not sit at meals but feel how well*
> *It soothed each to be the other by;*

The author of the book of criticism then wrote: 'The picture of Lorenzo and Isabella sitting at table and sensing their comfort for each other is as memorable as it surely is because it affirms sex's underground connection, even in the young and emotionally frantic, with a whole complex of tender instincts reaching back and back towards a well-being in which silence and a shared meal and a loved presence merge in the profoundest dreamlike peace.' Is that not beautiful? You can imagine how much this moved me, and how much I loved to see this written. Ah! this writer had written words I had never spoken. Sex's underground connection . . . and our memories from childhood, of a meal with our mother, in silence, rich with love. This is a complete explanation of love. I have never come across another to match it.

But then even more extraordinary than finding this very precise and incredibly acute observation (I was not aware in fact that the two qualities – precise and acute – ever did go together) was my discovery that someone had amended this passage, and actually improved upon it. At first reading I had come across what I thought was a blot, but as I read it through again I realised that one of the words had been crossed out with a fine pencil. The sentence which read, 'even in the young and emotionally frantic,' had been altered by a student to read, 'ESPECIALLY in the young and emotionally frantic.' This was too much; refinement of such a truth! For as I know, it is especially in the young and the emotionally frantic that these connections are made.

It inspired me that a student, nearby, suffered what I suffered, had amended the one slight weakness of this incredible passage. And that this unknown person – who I found so inspiring, who gave me such courage – was not her!

Dear Paul, I am so straitened by discovering the power of words, I hardly dare say I love you.

27th June

Dear Paul,

We all know it is better to give than to receive and like very much to see others obeying this precept. She is generous beyond belief. She gives everything she has. Time, money, are not the least of the things she hands out to whoever asks them. And the more she gives, the richer she is to me, to everyone. Ah! but how strange to see this, to see the beneficence of her generosity, its life-spreading qualities, the deep insistence she has on giving to people who do not matter as much to her as I. I believe there was never a more perplexing predicament for a baby like myself than to consider she will give everything to everyone, but will not give me love.

Dear Paul,

I wrote out on a scrap of paper those words I found in the book. I write them out several times each day. 'The picture of . . . and . . . sitting at table and sensing their comfort for each other . . . affirms sex's underground connection . . . with . . . tender instincts reaching . . . towards a well-being in which silence and a shared meal and a loved presence merge in the profoundest dreamlike peace.' My chief pleasure now is at table, with her and Tomas, eating a meal.

Today I was with Tomas and Kate, and one of the scraps fell out on to the table. 'What's that?' asked Kate. Tomas picked it up and read it. 'Something for Kate,' he said, and handed it to her. She read it and looked embarrassed. Tomas took it from her and gave it back to me. I have no way of telling if she looks as miserable when I am not there.

Paul,

The other day I came upon what Mary Shelley had written about her life after the death of her husband:

'What misfortune can equal death? Change can convert every other into a blessing, or heal its sting – death alone has no cure; it shakes the foundations of the earth on which we tread, it destroys its beauty, it casts down our shelter, it exposes us bare to desolation; when those we love have passed into eternity, "life is the desert and the solitude", in which we are forced to linger – but never find comfort more.' This was written sixteen years after Shelley's death.

What is remarkable about this passage is that all trace of consolation has been banished. Seldom does anyone who has suffered these pains fail to lie about it. How admirable Mary Shelley must have been. Hers is the only piece of writing on death I have ever read that would not be suitable for reading at a funeral.

So many things passed between us I never told you about, and I now regret not having done so. One was that Kate's flat was open always to anyone who was cold and hungry. Tramps would come by and knock on her door and be fed and sit by the fire. The unhappiest of these was Alec; the first time he came he sat himself down at our table – I think it was my birthday, and we had cooked a large meal together, and were enjoying it along with Frank – and on his plate Alec mixed soup, pancakes, cake, brown sauce, black pudding, rice pudding, tomato ketchup . . . There was such an abundance of foods – this is very much her way of celebrating . . . Alec, mixing them all together, raised an eye at our astonishment, and said blankly, 'It all goes down the same hole.' He never smiled, would whimper terribly; never was a man so gloomy. He once had a job as chauffeur to Compton Mackenzie, the writer, and lived with his wife in the basement of a fine townhouse beneath the great man, with little to do but polish up the car. But he never talked of this time without complaining about all the endless annoyances that bothered him. 'Oh she was such a nuisance,' he said of the housekeeper. There was no joy in any of his recollections . . . It seemed to me he was not aware of how far he had fallen. He would nick things from us, money, clocks, a brooch of Kate's, but what was worse was that he would bore us for hours about how wicked the world had become, how no one was trustworthy, how no one but his honest self had any virtue left in the world . . . These dreadful speeches were wrung like a sermon from him, he would sermonise through any interruption, looking at you with that awful look which said, if you don't listen, I will carry on twice as long as I intended.

Anyway, I tell you all this now because what happened today would not make sense if you did not know a little of the preamble . . . What happened today was that as I was walking across the Meadows I saw Alec in the distance. I was so pleased, I hurried up towards him, he was a link to a happier time. There was no way of knowing if he recognised me or not. He sat down on a bench and began to complain. He used to go, he said, to a kind woman, but he was not allowed in any more. We sat down on a bench together, I rolled a cigarette and offered him one, which he lit with a lighter that Kate had given me. 'Och, I've had it a long time,' he said. 'I wouldna' part with it for the world.' He was so much older and more decrepit than he had been a month ago, that I knew he would very soon be dead. He knew it too and complained in the same listless way of his approaching death as he had complained of everything in his life. 'Och, I'll be gone soon, right enough. Not that I mind.' It made me very sad that even death could wring no spark from his imagination.

For I have been thinking how love is like death . . . Both seize control from us, and it is only as we fall under their sway that we can appreciate anything in the world. As they deny us life they give us a taste of everything we could have enjoyed. I had a notion the other day that when we eat a strawberry yoghurt, the flavour of it has a taste of the longings and the regrets of a million dying souls. It is what they feel is the taste of life and youth.

You might remember I described a moment once, when I seemed on the verge of embracing my love for the first time. I had walked to see her at her mother's house, and we spent an ecstatic day and night together at her home, and then, very late, lying both of us on the floor, in that moment when we might have embraced each other and we did not, I threw my hands in the air and cried, 'I am so happy I want to die.' I never understood what prompted this . . . I think now that I knew I was never to be happier than at that moment. That instant's hesitation, that pause, told me of every pain that was to come, told me that love, as it blossomed, would be suffocated with suffering. It seems to me that no one can have been in such a confusion of joy and pain as I have been since that moment. If I have to die at all I wish I had died then. Not that I wish to die now. No, the reverse, to prove my love is eternal I am resolved to live forever.

Dear Paul,

The one relief for you since my troubles began is that I no longer pester you with recommendations to read various books. You put up with that nuisance very well, the Ossians, the letters of medieval students, etc. I apologise for all that. Having failed my exams, and your having done so well with all your scholarships, I wanted to show I was not hopelessly unfit to be your friend. And I thought that in an antiquarian exile I could overcome my shame at academic failure . . . Now this posturing means nothing to me, my studies are dead, I don't know what I do here and will soon leave. Books teach me nothing, my life and thoughts have become my own, as it were. I live in my head and search for the interesting thoughts, truths and beauties to be found there.

But last night I read a book, which I promise will be the last I recommend. It was *The Sorrows of Young Werther*, by Goethe. Two hundred years ago it was the most celebrated book in Europe. Now it is not much read, but if you would learn of a similar case to mine, then this book is that.

To read this novel was such an extraordinary event that I now feel composed for the first time in many weeks. The books I urged you to read I did not enjoy, I was pretending. Now I have been struck, physically struck, by a book and I cannot resist begging you read it. Maybe you know it, I had heard of it, but I had never heard anyone talk about it. It is impossible not to talk about it. My present confusion is abated by the desire to tell people about this extraordinary book . . . But of course, it is perhaps especially extraordinary to me, for it corresponds so closely to my recent experiences.

When I started to read this book I was from the first page reminded of my own passion and suffering. I held back the strangest tears; felt an intensification of my own grief, and also a consolation in seeing my pains so vividly described. I will give you a brief description of it.

A young man arrives in a country district in late-eighteenth-century Germany. He occupies himself by reading Homer, sketching and sending letters home. The first letters dwell on the limitations of provincial society, and his annoyance at the narrow conventions which rule every polite life. But he has heart and energy, and refuses to succumb to so low a level; he spurs himself to master his growing listlessness by roving ever further throughout the countryside. He extends a taste for landscape and develops an appreciation of the people, farmers and peasants, men and women, he finds there. He writes admiringly of the peasants he meets and talks to and marvels at the strength of their passions, their forbearance with the frustrations of their meagre life. He has a similar feeling for children. One evening he is persuaded to attend a dance. He sets off in a carriage of young women; on the way they are to stop and pick up another. One of the party coyly warns him that he must not fall in love with the girl they are about to collect, for she already has a sweetheart. The carriage stops outside the farmhouse, and Werther, curious about everything, walks in to collect the guest and discovers 'the most charming scene I had ever beheld'. The young woman is surrounded by her young brothers and sisters all demanding their bedtime slice of bread from their dear Lotte. Werther is captivated by the quality of affection between the old and the young. Lotte, who is about eighteen, is the eldest daughter of a recently widowed bailiff. A few months previously she had promised her dying mother to raise her siblings as if she were their natural mother. From the very first moment everything about Lotte inspires Werther, and confirms the justice of his most extravagant hopes. Just as Kate affected me, just as Kate redeemed the world for me, so Lotte does for Werther.

They dance that evening, and in between the dances they talk continuously. He visits her every day, and that growing sense of excitement and wonder never for an instant falters. The description of Lotte's beauty and character is so wonderful in itself, and corresponds so exactly with all my feelings for Kate, that I could not credit it. In many respects Werther is different from me, he is more intemperate, more direct, more articulate, more observant and more intelligent, but Lotte is my Kate. She is as beautiful and lovely as my Kate. (Paul, I am weeping as I write this. To write the words 'my Kate' fills my eyes with lovely tears.) With an exact copy of her kindness, an exact copy of her intelligence and penetration, an exact copy of her sympathy and conscience, and an exact copy of her betrothed. For this is the tragedy that causes all Werther's sufferings. Lotte is betrothed to a worthy young man called Albert, who is away on business and will soon return to be wed.

Ah! Can you imagine with what incredulity I read those pages! How like us were the lovers Lotte and Werther, compelled to be chaste, who loved but could only sympathise with each other. I felt for them more acutely than I felt for us; the happiness so soon swallowed in grief. I knew what it felt like, at last, to find another whose personality exposed to the sky the confirmation of all your most tender, most optimistic musings. Two beings who saw the same things, felt the same feelings, agreed on the meaning and value of truth and beauty and yet who could not profess their love. Lotte's vow to her mother prohibited any scandal; certainly it would have been the ruination of her brothers and sisters had she broken off her engagement to Albert. Incredible! a duty to a dead parent checked their love as it checked ours.

The poetic sympathy between them needed no frank words, their romantic attachment needed no confession, they understood each other perfectly when they danced together, when they looked upon a landscape together. I do not think this will sound corny to you, it is very beautiful, and a wonderful conception. I have lived the truth of it.

Albert returns, he learns that a young man has become a great friend of his betrothed. The two men are introduced, and form a friendship. Albert is very cordial to Werther, and Werther is very grateful for this, because it allows him still to visit his beloved Lotte. The three of them affect to be great friends. Lotte's feelings cannot be divined, except that she is made anxious by the growing wildness of Werther, whose outbursts against all convention increase in bitterness. Werther eventually has to leave them, the strain is too great. Lotte and Albert are married. Werther drives himself to find some new life and interest. He enters court and seeks a career in politics. It is hopeless, he knows what it is to be interested, to be involved in life, and the self-pretence of work disgusts him. He returns – he can do nothing else – there is a moment when he catches a glimpse of the married couple and thinks to himself they did not seem to be as happy together as he believed he and Lotte might have been. At that moment I could read no more. The tears that my absorption had held within me came out in a huge wail of grief. I cried as if I would never cry again. The agony of Werther's remote, discreet jealousy was both a balm and a scald.

From that point the identification was over. When Werther went out and killed himself I felt no sympathetic passion any longer. The suicide, which was the cause of the book's controversy, does not coincide with my version of the events. The ending of the book was a disappointment. I know that if the flush of love's pain carry us not straight to death, we live forever.

11th July

Dear one,

In a very little time I will put this sheet of paper in an envelope on which I will write your name. I will push it beneath your door, then I will walk to the train station.

I will take with me few things on the train. Most important to me will be three photographs I stole a long time ago from one of your boxes. You will not miss them. They are the fuzziest, the grainiest, the blurriest, the most indistinct ones I could find. Virginia's little lovebird is on your shoulder in one. In another a guitar is hanging on a picture hook. In all three a green silk scarf is wrapped around your head. An electric light is shining through your bunched-up hair, and dazzles to blindness an untidiness which can only be imagined! You are wearing your blue cardigan, and beneath that mossy wool, your lurex shirt glistens like chain-mail. I do not know who took these photographs, someone who was in your room one night, someone who did not know you, who did not love you, they are so fabulously indiscriminate.

I hope that once I am gone light and happiness will return to you.

I have in my heart one film of you I run again

and again and again. It is the way you tie a belt about your middle with such emphasis. Many hundreds of times each day I turn my eyes back and watch you binding your coat about your waist, turning and walking away with the insouciance of a young soldier. (Why is it such a stimulus to us both, this action of turning away? Why is it our strongest point of union?) Your shoulders and your back express such courage, such devotion to life and all the possibilities which life stretches before us.

I wish that I had longer to learn everything you could have taught me. I have determination, but no heart with which to enjoy life.

I seem to know everything that will happen to me. Grim paradox will rule my life: dejection will be elation, pain will be luxury, poverty will be boundless wealth, obscurity boundless glory and my new life a piece of marvellous quiescence. I know already that the sensation of leaving you far behind will feel to me like I am entering your body. That the exchange of the airs of the north for the stews of London will feel like a consummation of our love. I cannot help this madness or prevent myself from wallowing in all the austere consolations which solitude will bear up to me; but no matter, still it is right, still I am right; by diving low in the waters of oblivion I will keep for ever one part of all I have enjoyed of you and also the presentiment of lasting happiness.